Sweet Home

Carys Bray was awarded the Scott Prize for her debut short-story collection, *Sweet Home*. Her first novel, *A Song for Issy Bradley*, was chosen for Radio 4's *Book at Bedtime* and was shortlisted for the Costa First Novel Award and was winner of the Authors' Club Best First Novel Award 2015. She lives in Southport with her husband and four children.

Praise for *A Song for Issy Bradley*

'Bray demonstrates the comforts of faith – the magic, hope and imagination – as well as its restrictions. This is an impressive debut from a compassionate, wise and original new voice.'

Suzi Feay, *Independent*

'I started reading it and couldn't leave it alone . . . I cannot remember a time when a novel has seduced me so completely . . . Bray writes with such clarity, intelligence and authenticity that it feels as if a trusted old friend is telling you the story, that the characters are people you know . . . Bray displays warmth and real wit throughout despite the tragic content of this debut novel and the lean beauty of her writing makes it effortless to read.'

The Times

'Bray explores the healing power of religion with rare assurance in one of the year's most impressive debuts.'

Mail on Sunday

'I loved this tender, moving, funny and deeply truthful story about a family and a faith tested to breaking-point.'

Helen Dunmore, author of *The Lie*

'It's about faith, specifically religious faith, and what happens to that faith when the unimaginable happens. It's a good subject, rich and dramatic, and you realize, universal in ways you might not have suspected: we all have faith or whatever you want to call it . . . I loved *A Song for Issy Bradley*. It's wry, smart, human and rather miraculously, avoids mawkishness. And, ultimately, it's moving and comforting in a way that makes sense even to the agnostic.'

Nick Hornby, *The Believer*

'I don't remember the last time a book moved me to tears . . . a beautifully written, simple story of an all-encompassing religion which gives no comfort to the death of a child.'

Jenni Murray

'Bray performs a small miracle of her own by inhabiting each family member at every stage of the tragedy as their doubts and fears creep in . . . [and] manages it with an astonishing lightness of touch . . . A stunning, unmissable debut.'

Sunday Express

ALSO BY CARYS BRAY

A Song for Issy Bradley

Sweet Home

CARYS BRAY

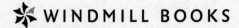
WINDMILL BOOKS

1 3 5 7 9 10 8 6 4 2

Windmill Books
20 Vauxhall Bridge Road
London SW1V 2SA

Windmill Books is part of the Penguin Random House group of companies
whose addresses can be found at global.penguinrandomhouse.com.

Penguin
Random House
UK

First published by Salt Publishing in 2012
First published in paperback by Windmill Books in 2016

www.windmill-books.co.uk

A CIP catalogue record for this book
is available from the British Library.

ISBN 9780099510628

Typeset in Weiss Std (12/16pt) by SX Composing DTP, Rayleigh, Essex
Printed and bound in Great Britain by Clays Ltd, St Ives Plc

MIX
Paper from
responsible sources
FSC® C018179

Penguin Random House is committed to a sustainable
future for our business, our readers and our planet.
This book is made from Forest Stewardship
Council® certified paper.

For Neil
For Alice, Joseph, Daniel and Sam
Wherever you are is home

Contents

Everything a parent needs to know   3

Just in case   15

Sweet home   25

The rescue   35

Wooden Mum   45

Dancing in the kitchen   59

Scaling never   61

The baby aisle   79

My burglar   87

The countdown   91

Bed rest   97

Under covers   111

Love: terms and conditions   121

The ice baby   137

Bodies   147

I will never disappoint my children   159

On the way home   165

Acknowledgements   179

Sweet Home

Everything a parent needs to know

Helen's daughter hates her.

'I hate you.' The words shoot out of Jessica's gap-toothed mouth. Helen would like to duck, but she laughs. It's a laugh that is arrested and immediately charged with impersonation: a whimper in disguise.

Jessica is pressed into the corner, each hand resting on a cool tile wall. The shrieks of other children echo around the pool and the chlorine-fogged air. 'I liked Daddy best,' she fires. 'I wish . . .'

Helen is porcupined by these articulated arrows. Nothing in all she has read can help her. She feels like an actress who has learned the wrong lines. She has rehearsed *Mary Poppins*, only to find herself appearing in *Night, Mother*.

> Never back your child into a corner. Always provide a way
> out and allow your child to save face. Humiliation can be
> extremely damaging for children. Avoid public humiliation
> at all costs.

> (*Everything a Parent Needs to Know: Two Hundred Steps to
> Familial Bliss* by DENISE GOODY)

Helen kneels, aware that she appears to be begging. She is begging. 'Come out of the corner. Don't stand there. Come and talk to me by the chairs.'

'No.'

'Well why don't you just get in the—'

'No.'

'If you just—'

'No.'

Helen fights another coil of laughter, this one cloaks tears. She is hot. The heavy, leisure-centre air is giving her a headache and the knees of her jeans are damp. She could roll them up, but she would rather have wet trousers than expose her raspberry-ripple legs. Jessica's head drops and Helen can see the knobble on the back of her neck through its almost transparent covering of pale skin and biro-fine veins.

'Look, Jess.' Helen gives herself eight out of ten for patience. 'Look. You said you wanted to wear Paul's old trunks. You said you didn't want to wear the swim suit.'

It is essential to respect your child's autonomy. Allow your child to make decisions and accept consequences. She will thank you for it.

(*Parenting for Idiots!* by JoAnn Humble)

Jessica moves her hands from the wall and clasps them tight in front of her. She has been drawing at school. There is felt tip on her fingers. Her drawings usually feature herself and Helen. Semi-circle heads grow straight out of boxy middles. Legs are pencil thin and over-long. Helen's face is often scribbled over. This is because it is usually raining or snowing in Jessica's pictures. It is nothing personal. Children don't really hate their parents. There are messages on the pictures. The messages are like tricks. Jessica recoils if Helen reads them incorrectly. Today's picture reads, *acisseJ morf mum oT*.

Without the protection of a costume, Jessica seems shelled. Her torso is buttery soft and pale. Her fine, mousey hair is jumbled into a pony tail. Paul's old trunks are blue and red. Helen holds the pink goggles. A small child's voice snakes though the air: 'Is that a boy or a girl?'

> The absolute, most important thing is to give a child a definite sense of who they are. Your child should feel comfortable with herself, happy in her own skin, certain of who she is.

> (*A Happy Childhood, a Happy Life!* by BRENDA JOLLY)

'Jessica, if you don't go over there to your class right now, I will be very, very cross.' Helen's voice wibbles, undermining her reported crossness. Another laugh wings her throat and she clips it to stop the tears that are fluttering close behind. 'Look,' she tries. 'You said you didn't want to wear your swimming costume. You found the trunks. You wanted to wear them.' Jessica's toes flex and tense again. 'So I said you could, but I wanted to bring the costume too, just in case. And then you said that I never listen to you. So I left the costume at home.'

Jessica stares at her feet. They are rigid. Toes curled, like claws. The other parents are watching. Helen can feel their stares between her shoulder blades. They will think, look at that poor girl whose mother has made her come swimming dressed like a boy. They will notice the crack of Helen's bottom peeping out of the top of her jeans as she kneels in the damp patch. Helen would like to reach around and pull her knickers higher, but she can't remember what kind they are.

Jessica raises her head slightly and glares out from under her fringe. Helen extends a hand, a come-on-this-is-enough hand, a let's-be-friends hand, and Jessica flinches, as if she is expecting to be hit. As if she is used to it. As if she can count on it. She is cornered, cowering and half naked. A tantrum would be better. A tantrum would involve an eye-rolling, we're-all-in-this-together glance at the other parents. It could be deflected by a shrug, a smile, and a when-will-she-grow-out-of-this chat in the changing room afterwards. But Jessica doesn't do tantrums.

When all else fails, think a happy thought. Like Peter Pan and Wendy, you won't soar unless you are happy. Remember a happy moment and grasp it as tightly as you would grasp your sword if you were to come face to face with an unfriendly dragon (no offence to any friendly dragons out there!).

(*Give a little whistle: Disney solutions to parenting challenges* by JO WHITE)

Helen's happy thought is that Dave from her adult-education class put his hand up last week to say that he had enjoyed doing The Whatsit of Alfred Prufrock. 'I relate to it,' he said. 'That stuff about walking in a room and wondering if people are looking at you. Getting it wrong and saying, "That's not what I meant." I thought it was all right, even though he's a bit of a tosser. He should eat the bloody peach and roll his trousers up if he wants to.'

Before Dave and his less appreciative classmates had made it down the echoing stairwell of the further-education college, Helen's imagination had given him sole charge of an aged mother and a life full of noble sacrifice as a dutiful, loving son. His mother would be waiting for him when he got home, Helen thought. When she heard the front door open his mother would shout, 'Is that you, our Dave?' And Dave would call, 'Yes, our Mam.' Then he would make her a cup of tea and sit next to her on the sofa. They would talk about his childhood. About how she always did her best and how he was grateful. Then Dave's mum, who actually had a name by this stage in Helen's invention – Phyllis – would put her arm around Dave and say, 'You're a good lad, all I ever wanted was for you to be happy. Now get that little book out, and read me another one of those funny poems by that George Eliot.'

Jessica whispers something, inaudibly.

'Say it again.'

'I want to go home.'

'Is this because of the trunks? It's fine if it is. It just seems to me that in the car, before we got here, you didn't really want to come. So I'm wondering if it's just the trunks?'

Jessica shrugs twice in quick succession. There have been so many swimming lessons. But she can't manage a length without a float. She thrashes and hammers at the water, fighting her way to the deep end. Occasionally the float pops out of her hands and she soaks into the water. Helen's stomach clenches as she waits for the teacher to slide into the pool and retrieve Jessica. He's always quick. But still . . .

Today in the car on the way to the pool Jessica had mumbled, 'I might need some help swimming.'

Followed by: 'Actually, I will need some help swimming.'

After that: 'Because I might have forgotten how to swim.'

And finally: 'I can't really swim.'

'That's why you're going, Jessica,' Helen had replied brightly. 'So you can learn how to swim.'

It is vitality important to introduce children to as many new experiences as possible. Like puppies, children need to be socialised. Children will not be afraid if they have been socialised correctly. They will approach life with the *joie de vivre* of a puppy.

> (*Like Dogs, Like Children: the new way to train your child* by BEN RUFF)

Helen stands. She gives up. Other parents drink too much, make promises they can't keep and hit their children. Helen gives up. Her feet have gone to sleep. They prickle as she walks toward the chairs where the other parents are sitting. Jessica follows several paces behind.

'Ah,' calls one of the parents. 'Ah, poor love.'

'Did you forget her costume?' another asks. 'Is that all they could find for you behind the desk?'

The changing rooms are quiet. Jessica puts her clothes back on ponderously. There is something heavy and cheerless in her, as if she was made for disappointment. She cultivates every hurt, every injury, and she wears them in the creases of her forehead, and in the tentativeness of her occasional embrace. Helen bends to help with her socks. Jessica's feet are soft and white, and her little toes curl like monkey nuts. Helen would like to kiss them.

'Remember when I was late for school in Reception Class, Mummy?'

'No.'

'Yes, you do. I couldn't find my cardigan, and you shouted at me, and I was crying when we got there.'

'No.'

'Well, I do.'

One day, Helen thinks, Jessica will sit on an orange, plastic chair in a designated room at a GP surgery and describe her horrendous childhood to a sympathetic counsellor. The trauma of attending swimming lessons wearing her older brother's trunks will equal her already misremembered recollections of the divorce. The counsellor will agree that her mother has ruined her life. This scene approaches with the inevitability of a speeding train.

'I'm sorry if I shouted at you when you were in Reception, Jess.'

'That's all right.' Jessica shrugs and examines the felt tip on her hands.

When they get home, Paul opens the door to them. 'You're early, Mum,' he says, caught red-handed with the Xbox controller. Fluff is growing on his upper lip and chin, but it cannot obscure the openness of his face.

'You obviously weren't expecting us.'

'How come you're back already?'

Helen relieves him of the controller as she explains.

'Doh!' He slaps his forehead. 'You Muppet, Jess!'

'Remember the story of Thumper,' Helen says. 'If you can't say anything nice . . .'

'Lol.' He grins.

'I don't think that's actually a word.' She smiles back at him.

'Lolz,' he says.

'That doesn't sound like a word, either. Go and do your homework.'

'Rofl,' he calls over his shoulder as he walks up the stairs.

'I think those are actually initials, not words,' Helen says. 'You can't really pronounce them like words because the vowels aren't—'

'Chillax, Mum,' he calls as he closes his bedroom door.

Jessica picks at her dinner. Her reasons for not liking food include it being too yellow, too soft and too runny.

'Remember when it was May Day at nursery, Mummy?'

'No. Eat your dinner, please, Jess.'

'Remember when it was May Day and everyone came with a May Day hat with ribbons on, to dance around the May Pole?'

'Not really.'

'Except me, cos you forgot.'

Helen remembers.

Paul laughs. 'OMG, that's nothing,' he says with his

mouth full. 'I remember once when Mum was an hour late picking me up from school because there was an accident on the coast road and she couldn't turn the car around or anything. She didn't have her mobile with her and no one knew where she was. Any more grub?'

Disappointment bounces off Paul like hail. He is amenable, unguarded, confiding. 'We did about boners in biology,' he said to her recently. 'Someone said that the Leaning Tower of Pisa is like a giant boner!' He laughed for a long time and eventually she had to join in. They stood in the kitchen together, giggling madly, until Jessica appeared in the doorway and drizzled sadness over the pair of them.

> The mother–daughter bond is the strongest, most loving tie of all. Girls need a loving, committed, attentive mother. With such a mother, what could possibly go wrong?!
>
> (*All you need is love!* by PAULINE MCCARTNEY)

At bedtime, Helen arms herself with fiction. 'How about this story, Jess?' she asks.

'No.'

'Or this one?'

'No.'

'How about you choose one yourself?'

'It's okay. We can have the one you wanted.'

'I was just making a suggestion, Jess. It's your choice.

What would *you* like?'

'No, it's okay, we can have the one you wanted. I don't mind.'

'Well I was hoping you would pick one that you like, so it would be more fun for you.'

'I'm trying to be kind, Mummy.'

'Sorry.' Helen reads Jessica a story about a dog. He runs away from home and gets so dirty that his family don't recognise him. They don't believe it's him until he's been in the bath. Then everyone hugs, and they are all happy. 'That's a lovely story, isn't it?' Helen smiles.

'I wanted *Nobody Likes Me*.' Jessica shrugs in a way that is meant to suggest not minding and minding very much all at once. 'The one where the boy's mum is horrible to him and he hides under the bed and falls asleep and dreams about—'

Helen bends to kiss the soft skin of her cheek.

'Ouch.' Jessica rubs her face hard with the flat of her hand.

'Sorry. I love you, Jess. Goodnight.'

'Goodnight, Mummy.'

Jessica has arranged her cuddly animals so that they are lying with their heads on her pillow. There is a small corner left for her. She rolls onto her side to make more room for the creatures, allowing herself a tiny wrap of duvet. And then she is still.

Later, after Paul has gone to bed, Helen reads. Tonight

she eschews help for happiness. She ignores the growing pile of hard-backed, hard-faced, hard-to-follow advice, and grasps her earlier happy thought.

It's dark outside when she falls asleep on the sofa, her head resting on the pages of a small poetry book. She dreams of Jessica's toes curled like claws, scuttling across the bottom of the swimming pool in the thick silence, oblivious to her poolside cries of, 'Time for you, and time for me, Jess.'

Just in case

I've been looking for a baby to borrow for a number of weeks. I've offered to look after several, even some I don't know very well. But their mothers seem suspicious. I ask nicely. I say please and I smile. I remember to ask whether it's a girl or a boy and how old it is, although I'm more interested in its length than anything.

This morning the lady who lives next door rang the bell. 'Emma! I didn't think you'd be here during the day, just called by on the off chance,' she said. 'Are you on holiday? Could you do me a massive favour?'

'I'm not on holiday,' I replied, rummaging through the pockets of my head, trying to find her name.

'My dad's got this pain in his chest. Mum's called an ambulance. I've got to meet them at the hospital.' She glanced at the baby in her arms. 'Only I really can't . . .'

I smiled carefully. 'I'd be happy to help.'

'Oh, thank you.' She handed the baby over. A little girl who might be the right size. 'I just want to make sure my dad's okay. I'll be straight back, probably no more than an hour. You'll be all right?' I nodded. 'We'll have to have you and Richard round for a drink again soon,' she called over her shoulder as she hurried to her car. And then she disappeared.

The baby was warm and sleepy. She arched and stretched as I carried her into the house, but she didn't wake up. I wonder if I should know her name. I sit on the sofa holding her.

When I was pregnant I was desperate to see inside my stomach. I thought of it as the ultimate, animate, travel case. I wished there was a zip I could open and close. The scan was thrilling, like one of those machines at the airport checking the contents of your luggage. Richard asked the nurse if she could tell the colour of the baby's hair. She wasn't sure whether he was joking. She told us it was a girl. When you are pregnant, people often ask if you want a boy or a girl. You must say that you don't mind. This is an unwritten rule. I know about unwritten rules.

'What do you want, Emma?' people asked me.

'I don't mind,' I said. But I wanted a girl.

When I'm not taking a couple of weeks off to get some rest, I work at Pack It In, a bag and luggage shop. I like my job. I like the warm smell of leather, the whispering crinkle of tissue paper, the snap of locks, and the soft crunch of zips. I like being the first to open a new bag. The first to discover the secretive slits in the lining that can hide credit cards or an iPod. The first to unsnap, unzip, undo every little compartment, and the first to unearth the tiny packet of guarding desiccant. I like the ding dong of the door every time it opens, and the initial impression of a customer, the sizing up which happens instantaneously. Does he need help? Is she just browsing? I recognise the awkward doorway pause of a man who is looking for a gift in unfamiliar territory. The furtiveness of serial browsers, the eagerness of handbag aesthetes, and the simmering anticipation of travellers, anxious to begin their holiday experience with new luggage.

Every bag, every case, is a receptacle for the hopes and aspirations of the person who eventually owns it. People carry all sorts in their handbags and luggage: passports, photographs, presents, treats, secrets too, in love letters, unpaid bills, appointment diaries and surreptitious cigarettes.

Every morning when I open the shop door, I am encircled by the welcoming smell of leather. Occasionally, I arrive early so I can enjoy the moment. There is something magical about a shop outside of opening hours. When Richard was small he used to imagine that he was locked in a supermarket overnight. Sometimes when we go grocery shopping he asks what I would do if I was locked in a supermarket.

'They're all open twenty-four hours now,' I said once. 'You couldn't be locked in.'

'Sundays,' he replied triumphantly. 'They open at

ten on Sunday mornings. You could be locked in on a Saturday night. What would you do? What would you *eat*? I'd probably start with the ice cream.'

'I'd rather be locked in Pack It In,' I told him. 'It'd be much nicer there. Warmer, cosier and the smell—'

'You're absolutely nuts,' he said.

My baby's name was Eve. After she was born I inched to my knees, ripped and stinging, to watch Richard cut the cord. Eve was bloody and scrabbling, bleating feebly, her eyes locked shut in the fluorescent hospital light. Unwrapped, revealed at last, and I couldn't believe that she was mine. I stayed in the hospital for a couple of days. There was a breast-feeding counsellor. She told you stuff about being a good mother. I wanted to be a good mother. Would you notice if your baby was unconscious, or would you assume that she was asleep? When I noticed, a doctor came, then another. They lifted Eve out of the cot and raced to a side room. I put my slippers on and followed. I held my breath as the tiny, manual pump squeezed oxygen into her mouth and nose. It seemed as if my bursting lungs might activate hers. If I didn't use any of the air, perhaps there would be enough left for her.

'Shit,' said the first doctor.

'Come on, darling,' the second urged.

It was probably only minutes before they stopped.

You might imagine that the moment of realisation is all hysterics and screaming. Pleading, howls, undignified bargaining, hasty promises and so on. Actors certainly seem to think so. But if I were an actor I would quietly say, 'Oh.' That's what people really do.

'How could you not *notice?*' Richard asked when he arrived, half dressed and terrified. He hasn't mentioned it since, except to say I must be more careful in future and he doesn't blame me.

Afterwards my arms felt empty. Richard bought me a Gucci bag. The long strap sat between my breasts and their constant dribble of milky tears. I went back to work early, my bra stuffed with wads of tissue. There was a sign in the bin. It said, 'Eve – 8lbs 2oz. Congratulations Emma!' I wondered how many people had walked past and seen it. What had they thought? I told Phil, the manager, that I would lock up. I stuck the sign back in the window. I went outside and walked backwards and forwards, pretending to be someone else.

Eve. What a lovely name, I thought.

Eight pounds is a good weight, I thought.

A girl. Lucky Emma, I thought.

When I had finished, I put the sign in the bin and locked the door.

After I'd been back for a few weeks, a woman came into Pack It In. She was going on holiday. She wanted to buy luggage. In her newspaper there was a story about a man who had found a suitcase when he was clearing out his late mother's loft. Inside the suitcase was a baby skeleton. That's what the woman said. A *baby skeleton*. As if it might grow into an adolescent skeleton and then an adult skeleton. Phil interrupted her. He told her not to believe everything she read in the paper, and he pretended that we were about to close for lunch. Then he gave me the afternoon off.

I wondered what kind of suitcase the baby skeleton was found in. Say it was born in the 1960s – it might have been hidden in a soft-bodied case. Something classic with a teal, brown and green floral pattern and a leather base, handle, and trim. A case like that would have silver zippers and a lined interior, with separate sections and tie downs. Or perhaps the baby skeleton was hidden in a more modern model, like the Antler Zenith, with a red moulded shell and grey interior. The Antler Zenith had flush fitting locks. The base and lid had an ottoman lining, like a quilt.

Eve's coffin had a quilted interior with a lacy pillow. It had silver handles. She wore a white dress and a bonnet to cover the stitches. They opened her head in the post-mortem, like a lid. I had to sign a form. They did blanket stitch. It wasn't neat. The stitching on my Gucci bag is straight with high-quality threading; only replica bags have lopsided, inconsistent stitching. I dressed her myself. She was raw-meat cold because the undertaker kept her in a refrigerator. There was a story on the news of a man who reached into his baby's coffin for a goodbye kiss, only to discover that it was alive. This happened in India. Eve was dead. She was too cold to kiss.

I tried not to think of her underground, decaying in the thick, damp silence. Then I read that the decomposition of the human body is a cascade process. There are four stages: fresh, bloat, decay and dry. I don't like the word *cascade*. It makes me think of skin and tissue streaming off in a pulpy torrent. I'd rather imagine the flesh wisping away like dandelion seeds, leaving slender bone stems behind. It's possible that the baby skeleton in the woman's newspaper was partially mummified. I know because I looked it up. The bodies of newborns that have never ingested food lack the internal microbial flora which initiates decomposition. These bodies quite commonly mummify if kept in moderately dry conditions.

'If you could go anywhere at night, and do anything, where would you go?' I asked Richard one evening.

'The supermarket, of course.'

'I'd go to the cemetery and dig Eve up.'

'You bloody wouldn't.'

'No, you're right,' I said. 'I'd never dig her up.' Grave diggers go on a week-long residential course. They have to learn to use a JCB. I read about it. There's no way I could dig her up by myself.

'That wasn't funny, Emma.'

'I wasn't trying to be funny.'

'Perhaps we should try again?'

I said I'd think about it.

I started collecting the desiccant after I bought the suitcase. Phil gave me a discount on the case. He said it would do me good to go on holiday and offered to give me time off at short notice if I found a last-minute deal. I chose the small Samsonite Termo Spinner, in lavender. It's made of high-strength polypropylene and has a ten-year global warranty. Someone has registered a patent for an airtight suitcase, but you can't buy one yet. I checked. As I unpacked the bags at work, I borrowed the desiccant. There are thirty-eight packets of desiccant in the interior pockets of my Samsonite case. It is an extremely dry environment.

Last week a customer we hadn't see for a while came into Pack It In. Her name was Angie Proctor.

'Emma!' she said. 'I saw the notice months ago. Belated congratulations! What did you call her again? I know you had a little girl, but I can't remember—'

'Eve.'

'Ah, yes.'

'She's dead.'

Phil strode out from the behind the counter as Angie Proctor's eyes filled with mortified tears. 'I'm afraid Emma lost little Eve.'

'I didn't lose her,' I said. 'She's not been carelessly misplaced. She's dead.'

Angie Proctor remembered that she was late for an

appointment. After the door shut behind her, Phil asked me to take a couple of weeks off. To rest.

This baby does not look like Eve. She is definitely conscious. I can tell because I am watching her stomach move up and down. I am being careful. This is how I might have sat with Eve. Nearly lunch time on a Wednesday. Doing nothing in particular. When she died Eve was not much smaller than this baby is now.

The Samsonite suitcase is waiting in my bedroom. The baby keeps sleeping as I carry her up the stairs. I place her gently on the bed, so as not to wake her. I lift the suitcase alongside her. The size is perfect. This is what I needed to know. I open the lid and place her on the silky lining inside. Just to see. This is what I should have done with Eve. I should have kept her, like a secret. A Tollund baby in a suitcase. But Eve's skin and tissue are cascading into the earth. Rotting into her bonnet and dress. Staining the tiny lace pillow. She is shrinking into a baby skeleton. Richard wants to try again, and I can't say yes until I have made the arrangements. Just in case.

I want to feel it, that moment of surprise as the case is opened and its secret revealed. I snap the lid closed. It isn't airtight. She should be all right. But perhaps I should count to thirty as a precaution. Thirty seconds shouldn't do any harm and she is asleep. She won't know anything about it. It's probably very comfy in there. Should I begin at number ten now? If I begin counting at ten will that account for the time already passed, or should I start at fifteen? Lavender was the right choice. I want a girl, but I will be careful not to say that to anyone. You mustn't actually say it. It's one of those things you mustn't say. Like dead. You mustn't say that your baby is dead because it upsets people. Perhaps I should start counting at fifteen . . .

The click of the front door interrupts my counting.

'Emma? Where are you?' Richard calls. He takes the stairs two at a time, slowing as he reaches the bedroom. 'Ta-dah! Surprise!' He comes to stand behind me and brushes warm lips against the back of my neck. 'It's lunch time and I'm *hungry*.'

His hands trace the arc of my vacant stomach and he nudges the backs of my legs with his, encouraging me to move forward. But I stand still as he embraces me, my eyes fastened on the suitcase, so beautiful on the bed, snapped shut around its precious secret.

Sweet home

Of course no one accused the old woman of being a witch. But she was foreign. Her words percolated up the tunnel of her throat, espresso-thick and strong. Bad weather had eroded her face. Some believed that the sun had crisped her skin into coriaceous pleats. Others blamed the chaw of a wintry climate. No one knew where she had come from, though lots of people privately thought that perhaps she ought to go back.

There was no interest in the small parcel of woodland until the old woman bought it. The wood grew at the edge of the village, at the brink of awareness. For most people its existence was an abstract or fleetingly pleasant local detail. After the old woman's visit to the estate agent, everyone suddenly began to talk about conservation. They shook their heads and tutted as they wrapped their mouths around unfamiliar words like heritage and legacy. Remarks about the wellbeing of red squirrels and dormice speckled habitual conversations about the weather, and people became overnight experts on the preservation of indigenous wildflowers. There was speculation that ghost orchids and wild gladiolus grew in the wood, leading to claims that it should have been categorised as an Area of Outstanding Natural Beauty, and its sale accordingly prevented.

Following the completion of the sale, the old woman bought a tent from the camping shop on the high street. Then she trudged down the B road to her new acquisition. She was followed, several days later, by a foreign removal truck, leading people to mutter darkly about planning permission and residential dwellings. A few especially indignant individuals pursued the truck. They stood at the edge of the wood and watched the tail lift lower to reveal a colossal, black, antique stove, crouching fatly on ball and claw legs. Three men emerged from the back of the truck and, along with the driver, moved the stove onto the woodland floor. The tail lift was raised and lowered a second time to reveal several sacks of flour, numerous Tupperware containers, a stepladder, an axe, a shovel and a chicken coop.

During the days that followed, everyone kept an eye on the B road. They were disappointed not to observe flatbed lorries stacked with building supplies, speedy white trade vans or even a removal truck containing the rest of the old woman's possessions. Although no such vehicles were observed, the old woman's intentions were perfectly plain and people were clearly obliged to report her to the authorities.

The Planning Office couldn't cope with the volume of phone calls. Public-sector redundancies had culled all but one of the secretaries and she didn't have either the time or the inclination to politely log numerous versions of the same complaint. After ten similar objections, the phone was switched to answer machine and a Planning Officer was despatched to investigate as a matter of urgency.

The Planning Officer wasn't one to talk. But on his way back from the wood he stopped off at the pub for a drink and felt he ought to reveal that the old woman was indeed planning to build. However, as the structure would not be permanent, there was nothing he could do about it. He was also compelled to disclose that the old woman had applied for a coppice grant worth £500, money which would surely be better spent on honest, hardworking, English people. And while he had a captive audience, he made an eloquent speech about the inadequacies of the government. When he'd finished he called a taxi because he was a responsible drinker: he'd claim for it later on expenses.

The old woman built her house around the stove. She dug out the foundations with a shovel and filled trenches with slow-baked slabs of salt dough and buckets of oozy sugar paste. She cooked thick gingerbread bricks and glazed them with glacé icing which set hard during the cool, wood-shaded evenings. Paper-thin slices of gelatine were latticed into windows, criss-crossed by steady cords of ganache. She constructed a roof out of Linzertorte squares and piped meringue along every join. The midday sun hardened the egg-white mortar into stiff, crispy peaks. When she had finished, she sat on her gingerbread porch modelling tiny flowers out of fondant. She dyed them using wild onion skins, beetroot, and hollyhock petals, and placed them in gingerbread window boxes.

It was only when the postman had to deliver a package addressed to The Gingerbread House, using a postcode which indicated the wood at the margin of the village, that people heard about what the old woman had done. They chatted about it in the Post Office, discussed it in the pub and then sauntered down the B road on the pretext of getting some fresh air. The gingerbread house was set back from the road by several hundred feet, but was just about visible from the path through the criss-cross of foliage and branches. A crowd gathered at the edge of the wood, their exclamations rising in a whip-swirl of disquiet.

'It looks like gingerbread.'

'You don't think she's a . . .'

'She should have used an English recipe.'

'Like shortbread.'

'I don't think shortbread—'

'Or Swiss roll.'

'Isn't Swiss roll from—'

'Victoria sponge, then. You can't get more English than that.'

'It's not in keeping with the character of the village.'

'Is this a conservation area? Are we in a conservation area? Maybe the Planning Officer can make her take it down.'

'I don't think so. He said not. Although I doubt he realised that she was intending *this*.'

'It's unhygienic. Don't you think it's unhygienic? It'll attract mice and rats.'

'I bet she won't pay council tax.'

'How about home insurance?'

'What could she insure it against – compulsive eaters?'

'I need a drink, anyone up for a quick half?'

It would not be true to state that everyone grew used to the gingerbread house. However, it did become a hard fact of people's existence, like gastritis or heartburn. The old woman often walked along the B road to the high street and back again, carrying supermarket carrier bags packed with butter, sugar and glycerine. She walked slowly, the 's' of her spine concertinaing into a tortile 'z' as she hefted her shopping. Occasionally people passed her, but no one offered to help.

In the weeks and months that followed, no one's milk

soured. No one's allotment crop failed and the weather was typical of early and subsequently late autumn. But as winter approached, the Post Office closed down and the highspeed broadband connection date was postponed. In the week before Christmas, the sky tipped a foot of snow over the village and hundreds of condensing boilers failed. In the New Year, VAT went up to 20%. And everyone began to see a pattern in the configuration of events, began to believe that the old woman's arrival had catalysed their misfortunes.

The quiet in the wood was welcome and calming. The passage of time was determined by the seasons rather than hours and minutes. The old woman found that she was pleasantly busy. Every day she tended to her chickens, chopped logs for the stove and maintained and repaired her house. The heavy snowfall limited her activities, and trips to the supermarket were suddenly difficult. But the stove belted out plenty of heat, and she watched the flames osculating like tongues behind its wide glass mouth as she relaxed in her lebkuchen chair.

It was after the snow began to melt that the old woman noticed the damage to her house. She was on her way out to the supermarket to look for blocks of insulating marzipan in the January sale, when she observed that the decorative sugar work on the external lintels had been removed. She paced the perimeter of the house and discovered that caramelised sugar swirls had been broken off the window shutters. Gumpaste flowers and butterflies had been disconnected from the fondant ivy and several gingerbread bricks had nibbles gnawed out of them.

The old woman made her way along the B road to the high street. It was hectic in the supermarket. Everyone was busy buying lots of reduced-price items they desperately needed. The old woman filled a basket with slabs of discounted marzipan and joined the long queue for the checkout. When it was almost time for her to pay, she turned to address the line of customers behind her.

'Please tell your children to stop vandilisationing my house.' The old woman's words rattled out of her throat, colliding with people's ears.

'She's definitely German,' someone whispered. 'Only a German could invent such a long word. And they don't know how to behave in queues, either.'

'Do you have any proof?' one of the shoppers asked.

'Our children wouldn't do such a thing,' said another.

'Even if they did, you couldn't blame them. Everything's so expensive. With the Post Office gone there's nowhere to buy penny sweets.'

'And it's partly your fault,' a fourth bargain-hunter accused. 'Are you trying to lure the kids to your house, or what?'

'You are rationalisationing,' the old woman replied. 'What if I was to shatter-smash *your* houses?' The clatter

31

of her consonants caused shoppers who weren't in the queue to turn and stare.

'It's not a proper house, anyway,' someone called bravely from the cigarette kiosk as the old woman paid and left the shop.

Everyone remembered the old woman's outburst the following week when two children went missing: they rehearsed her aggression and her threatening behaviour. Of course, no one knew how the story landed on the front page of the *Daily Mail*, alongside a photograph of the old woman's grizzled face. The children were found. However, their short-lived absence tailed the old woman, and people buttressed their dislike of her with fear.

The quiet in the wood was heavy and deadening. The old woman stayed indoors as much as possible, despite her need for materials to repair the escalating vandalism to her property. She ventured outside to chop logs, but otherwise kept warm by the stove, calling out a precautionary, 'Go away' every so often.

She didn't hear the children approach. She heard the soft snaps as fondant flowers were plucked from her window box. She rose to her feet and opened the gingerbread door. Outside a boy and girl were gobbling the delicate decorations.

'I wish you would not be eating my house,' she said. 'Please, go away.'

The children paused to consider her.

'People are scared of you,' the boy said, cautiously.

The old woman nodded.

'You *are* a bit strange,' added the girl.

'Are you a wicked witch?' the boy asked.

'No.'

'You're just a very wrinkly woman, then,' he said, and he stepped up to the front door where he snapped a cylinder of frosting from its frame. 'Your house is yummy.'

Anger expanded into the old woman's chest where it swelled like yeast. She grabbed the boy by his shirt, tumbling him into the house. 'You will no longer ever be eating my house.'

The girl stepped inside, following her friend as he attempted to scramble to his feet. Both children looked alarmed. The old woman felt pleased. She opened the stove door for fright, for emphasis. Hot air leapt out at the three of them.

'If you come again I will roast you,' she blustered.

No one knows what happened next. The children maintained that they ran away, terrified by the old woman's threat. Newspaper headlines mentioned sticky situations and just desserts. The police report described an ill-fated tumble, a terrible accident. It was all very sad. People tried not to talk about it. It was easier that way. It meant that no one had to wonder whether having osmosed the prevailing sentiment, the children simply pushed the old woman into her stove.

The rescue

The supermarket glows like a sprawling lighthouse in the darkness of the empty car park. The father approaches the entrance and finds a trolley to lean on. As he walks, he catches glimpses of himself in reflective surfaces. Eye bags dip past his cheek bones. They are puffed with the unrealised hopes of constant Googling. Sometimes he does not recognise his reflection in the mirrored glass and metallic fittings, sometimes he feels sorry for the jaded, old man reflected there. He shuffles past the newspaper stand and turns left. He browses the greetings cards, looking for one that he might send to the son. But nothing will do. He trundles aimlessly down the electrical aisle, wondering if the son still has the new kettle. Perhaps he should buy another, in anticipation of the new kettle's inevitable disappearance. Or perhaps he should buy a microwave to replace the one that vanished last year. It would be a great relief to know that the son might eat something hot, if only for a matter of days or weeks. The father likes to imagine that there is *something*, either on the internet or in the supermarket, that will jog the son's memory and rescue him from the world he began to inhabit twenty years ago. It is just a process of elimination, he tells himself. But secretly, in the grotto of his heart, he knows that he is engaged in a much harder operation.

In the beginning he thought the rescue would be easy. Equipped with a *Say-No-to-Drugs* book and audiocassette, he set out to winch the son to safety.

'Just say no,' he pleaded.

The son laughed. 'Oh fuck off, Dad,' he said.

'We aren't the kind of people who say fuck off to each other,' the father protested, before he understood that there are worse things than words.

There were more books; books that alternately blamed and encouraged the father. The books all agreed on one thing: the son had to reach rock bottom before things would get better. The father thought that they had reached rock bottom when the son dropped out of college and didn't take his A levels, despite being predicted a B in maths. Remembering this makes him laugh. His past expectations tickle him like a dry cough.

He thought they were at rock bottom when the son stole five hundred pounds from the mother's bank account. He thought it again when the son set fire to the house, and when the son borrowed the car and crashed it. The father was certain they were at rock bottom when the son was admitted to the psychiatric hospital, and he followed the nurses around, telling them that the son used to be good at maths in order to give them some idea of the man they were about to rescue.

When the son became homeless the father was convinced that things couldn't get worse, and then the council housed the son in the basement flat of a block inhabited by social misfits and other drug addicts. Every subsequent, incremental worsening of the son's life over the intervening years has led the father to think *this* is it, we are here, at last. And he has settled in, set-up camp, made accommodations and looked for the positive. There is *nothing* worse than death, he thinks. Where there is life, there is hope, he thinks. There has to be. There is. He won't have it that there's not. He is still following every degree of the son's slide to this elusive, final destination, after which The Rescue will assuredly take place.

There *are* worse things than death, thinks the mother as she awakes to discover cool, empty sheets where the father ought to be. She lies with her eyes shut for a few moments, trying to trick herself back to sleep, but it's no use. *This* is worse than death, she thinks. If the son were dead she would have her memories, but pictures of the man he is are supplanting images of the boy he was, and even her former happiness is unravelling. She wishes that she could start again, disentangle or unpick the son, like a piece of needlework. Like one of the kitschy cross-stitch samplers she used to enjoy making with little sayings on:

CARYS BRAY

You are my Sonshine and *Don't wait to make your son a great man, make him a great boy.* The son is her handiwork, her life's work, and she doesn't even like him. His front teeth are grey-brown and perforated. She cries over silly things like his teeth. She wants to say, 'I drank a pint of milk every day when I was pregnant so that you would have good teeth, and I don't even like the bloody stuff.'

When he was small, the son used to sit on her knee while he watched television. If she tried to get up, he would hold her arms tight, fasten them about his trunky, little waist and say, 'Watch me, Mummy! Watch me watching.' She cannot watch him any more.

There is solace in the twenty-four hour news channels. Whatever the atrocity, she thinks of the mothers: high-school shootings, riots, stabbings, and suicide bombers. Oh, their poor mothers, she thinks. At least *her* son isn't a murderer or a rapist. At least he has only ruined his parents' lives. She often wakes to an empty bed on Fridays and Saturdays, but occasionally the father also makes nocturnal excursions during the week. He says that he pops to the supermarket. But she knows he visits the son as well. She observes the changes in his vital signs: the wretchedness before the visits; the flatlining afterwards, and she is ready with defibrillating cups of tea on his return.

The father manoeuvres his trolley out of the electrical aisle and pauses to stare at a crowd of store employees

38

gathered around a television display. He can see from the banner scrolling across the bottom of the screens that they are watching a twenty-four-hour news channel. He edges toward the crowd.

'What's going on?' he asks a lad with an enormous hole in his earlobe.

'It's the rescue,' the lad says.

The father doesn't watch the news. He can't understand why the mother bothers with it: depressing, miserable information from all over the world, brought straight to your front room by eager journalists, who would probably begin each report with 'Guess what?' if they could get away with it.

'What rescue?'

'You know. The miners. From Chile. They're about to bring the first one up.'

He has a vague awareness of this story. The mother has mentioned it, he thinks. The lad with the holey ear steps to one side, making space for the father to watch.

The Chilean landscape is lunar, otherworldly. Men in hard hats and puffer jackets are clustered around a bright yellow A-frame. The camera focuses on the ground and the father can see the black edges of a large pipe poking out of the earth like the sides of a dustbin. A cable is winding out of the hole, up and around a cartwheel at the top of the frame, like a giant fishing reel. It is as if they are attempting to angle the miner out of the earth.

Eventually, a torpedo-like capsule appears. The assembled crowd clap and cheer and the camera moves to focus on the contorted face of a small boy; it's all too much for him and his sobs carry over the applause.

The lad with the holey ear wipes his eyes. 'It's one of those moments, isn't it?' he says. 'Like 9/11 or Elvis dying. People will remember where they were when this happened.'

The father nods, uncertainly. The capsule is opened and the first miner steps out wearing sunglasses, a red hard hat and a cautious smile. The whistles and cheers resume, but the cries of the miner's son are again discernible as he rushes to embrace his father.

'Back to work, then!' The lad with the odd ear smiles and follows his colleagues toward the bakery, where heaving trolleys are waiting to be unloaded.

The father stays in front of the televisions. He listens to discussions of the miners' sixty-nine-day captivity, to accounts of what they have been eating and descriptions of the conditions a mile below the earth's surface. He decides to watch the second rescue. It's not often that something nice happens on the news. Afterwards, he will buy something edifying for the son, and then he will go home and have a bit of a snooze before work.

The second miner is quite a character. He cheers and shouts and repeatedly hugs the Chilean president. The father smiles as he watches. I'll just stay for one more, he thinks. He will be especially tired at work, but what can they do about it? He's only two years off retirement. After the third miner emerges, the father decides that he has time to watch the fourth and cautiously removes a dining chair from a display in the central aisle. He sits down in front of a television with the empty trolley at his side.

The mother climbs out of bed and explores the carpet with tentative, slipper-finding feet. Downstairs, she fills the kettle, switches on the television, and is suddenly glad to have woken. She sits on the sofa with a steaming mug of tea and watches as the fourth miner is freed. She has a little cry, calls herself a silly old cow, and boils the kettle again in preparation for the fifth rescue.

The fifth man is the youngest, she learns, as she flattens a teabag with the back of her spoon. His mother will be delighted, she thinks. She sits down again and waits for the rescue capsule to surface. It is almost eight o'clock in the morning. The father will be late for work if he doesn't come home to get ready soon. She wonders exactly how long he has been gone and what he has bought. She is angry with him. She is sorry for him. And it is at moments like these that she despises the son. It has been a surprise to realise that her love is not elastic, that it doesn't stretch as far or run as deep as the father's; he still talks about rescue and rehab, still believes that

41

change is possible. But no one can force the son. He has human rights, even though what is left of him is hardly human at all.

At eight o'clock, the lad with the holey ear comes back. 'Finished my shift,' he says. 'Can't believe you're still here. Are you all right?'

'Last one,' says the father. 'Then I'm off home.'

'What number is this?'

'Number five. The youngest of them all. He's just a boy, really.'

They watch the television in companionable silence. The cable twists up from the depths of the earth and out of the dustbin-width of pipe. Finally the rescue capsule emerges. The excitement of the miner's father is palpable, his smile joyous. Father and son embrace.

The holey-eared lad blinks tears away. 'I'm going home to watch the rest of it,' he says.

The father nods to him and gets up from the borrowed dining chair. He leaves it next to the empty trolley and walks outside into daylight. If he hurries he can get home in time to change for work. But he doesn't go home. He drives across the city to a concrete tower block. He parks on the double yellow lines outside and, ignoring the keypad at the entrance, gives the reinforced door a shove. It opens as he knew it would. The tenants always leave it unlatched. He approaches the concrete stairs and begins the walk down, below ground level. The stairwell smells like a multi-storey car park. Piss stains and needles decorate each landing.

The son lives at the very bottom. The corridor that leads to his flat is long and cavernous. Two fluorescent light strips are bolted to the ceiling. One is smashed, the other sputters dimly. When he reaches the son's door, he stops. The door is blue and it's stained in one corner with a fine spray of what looks to be blood. Obscenities are scrawled over it in permanent marker, and the number has been broken off. He could probably kick the door down. If he really wanted to, he could boot it off its hinges, storm inside, and drag the son from his bed, or the sofa, or the floor. He could haul the son's bony frame over his shoulder, climb the concrete staircase and bundle him into the car. But he doesn't. He steps back until his spine touches the solid corridor wall, and then he edges to the floor. The cold of the concrete seeps through his trousers, as he waits in the shadows for someone to rescue his son.

Wooden Mum

At night, after I put Tom and Letty to bed, after I finish
sitting outside Tom's bedroom door to stop him coming
downstairs, after I finish telling him not to switch the light
on, and not to strip the bed, after he stops laughing and
banging the wall with his fist, when he is finally asleep, I
go downstairs to tidy up. His cars ring the perimeter of the
lounge. Sometimes they are ordered by colour, sometimes
by model, sometimes by imperceptible nuances invisible
to my neurotypical eyes. I put them away and close
up Letty's dolls' house. There are often cars in the tiny
dolls' kitchen, sitting at the table opposite the wooden,
cotton-haired boy and girl. Sometimes there's a Dalek in
the living room, behind the sofa where wooden Dad sits,
oblivious. I search for wooden Mum who is frequently
not in either of the first-floor bedrooms. I open the roof
and check in the nursery. There are times when the cot
leans, balanced precariously on a pile of quilted dolls'
bedding, and wooden Mum is hidden underneath. There
are times when she is lying in the bath under a jumble
of tiny towels or crouching in the wooden dog's kennel.

I rescue her and put her to sleep in the master bedroom. She always looks pleased because Letty has cut a gory, biro smile into her round, peg face.

I am usually cheerful. Mostly reconciled to things. There are two occasions when I remember crying. The first was in the car, at the top of Fore Street after driving the babysitter home. I had to pull over. Once I could see again, I wiped my nose on my sleeve and drove home. My face was dappled and streaked with mascara. I ploughed straight up the stairs, passing Stuart on the landing. He was on the phone to his mother.

'I'm going to bed.' My voice jellied around the words.

'You got what you wanted,' he replied, placing his hand over the telephone mouthpiece. 'You got your label. Hope you're happy.'

I ignored his contempt. He ignored my streaky cheeks and parched eyes.

The other occasion was yesterday evening before the putting away of Tom's cars, before the coaxing of bedtime. It happened when Stuart got home from work and I started to tell him about the sign in Tom's classroom. The sign must have been there all term. I noticed it at home time yesterday because Tom forgot his lunch bag, and I slipped into the classroom to help him find it. The sign is on the wall above the teacher's desk, next to a photograph of Tom. In the photograph he is wearing a blue plastic apron and holding a paintbrush. Behind him an easel grips another of his entirely green paintings. The person who was taking the picture must have shouted, 'Smile!' But the sweet-wrapper twists at the corners of his mouth don't negate Tom's frown. The accompanying sign reads, '*My name is Tom Parsons. I have Asperger Syndrome. I have behavioural problems.*' A smaller, unrelated sign below says, '*In order to promote the children's self-esteem we do not correct spellings or use red pen.*'

'There's a sign on the wall in Tom's classroom,' I said as Stuart shrugged out of his coat and lifted the lid of a pan on the stove. 'Tom thinks it says he's got a nut allergy. I asked him about it when we got home. He must have been wondering why it's there, why they've got it wrong.'

'Well tell them he hasn't got an allergy. Simple.'

'It's not about that at all. It says . . .' A series of noises vaulted out of my mouth. Wobbly, frightening noises that hung in the air with the steam from the stove. Stuart stared. Tom poked his head around the door.

'Off you go.' Stuart moved in an effort to hide me. 'Off you go, Tom. Go on. Dinner's not ready. Mum's upset. Go and play cars. Off you go. Now.' He pulled my face into his shoulder. 'Shush. Shush. God! Shush. It's only a sign. What are you crying for? You silly thing. It's nothing to cry about.'

My nose ran. So did my mascara. I cried all over his white shirt. I expect it's ruined.

*

This morning we will probably be late. There's no winner in the race to school, but there are definitely losers. Groups of parents linger at the gate chatting. Latecomers have to run the gauntlet of jokes. Late ones coming through! Did your mum sleep in again? School starts at nine! Run, run!

I can't find Tom's tie. I keep telling myself that I should ask him to pass it to me in the car on the way home from school, but I get distracted. There's no pattern in the discarding of his tie, he just takes it off and drops it. It could be in the bathroom. It could be outside.

'Letty, can you help me look for Tom's tie?'

'Oh, Mummy,' she yells from the lounge. 'I'm watching *Newsround*.'

'Letty, please.'

'Why should I? It's not my tie. And Tom's bigger than me. Why can't he look for it himself?'

Tom wanders into the kitchen with a fire engine in his hand.

'Where's your tie, Tom?'

'Dunno.'

'Why haven't you got your shoes on?'

He shrugs.

'When did you last have it?'

'What?'

'Your tie.'

'Nee-nah,' he mutters and he holds the fire engine up to his face, spinning a wheel with his index finger.

I go outside to look for his tie in the car.

Tom was diagnosed in a private hospital. It was expensive. Stuart said it would be worth it to prove that there was nothing wrong, nothing that some decent discipline couldn't solve. 'Where will Tom be while we're talking about him?' I asked when I booked the appointment over the telephone.

'Don't worry, a nurse will be playing with him,' the receptionist said.

The nurse gawped at us while we answered the doctor's questions. She sat on the floor next to Tom, ignoring him. He kicked her, softly, an exploratory sort of kick.

'Well, I'm not playing with you now,' she said.

'You weren't anyway,' he replied.

As we stood to leave, the doctor said fish oils are a waste of time, behaviour management doesn't work and support at school is unlikely because he's not stupid enough.

'The doctor said that one day Tom might get a job at Tesco,' I told the babysitter as I drove her home.

'That's great news, Mrs Parsons,' she said.

The doctor had smiled as he said it, as if he'd just bestowed a consolation, like the good fairy in *Sleeping Beauty*.

*

I can't find Tom's tie in the car. He's waiting for me at the front door.

'Is it there?' he asks.

'Nope,' I say and point to the visual timetable on the back of the door. 'Shoes, Tom.' He gets his shoes out of the rack and Velcroes them on. I move my index finger along and point to the laminated picture of a school bag. 'Where's your bag?'

'Dunno,' he says, and bolts for the stairs.

The visual timetable was supposed to help. I went on a course. Chronic disorganisation and an inability to focus on uninteresting things are supposedly typical. Visual timetables are the solution. The course leader was adamant. 'What he needs is a visual timetable,' she said.

'But he can read these short words, so surely if I just write them—'

'He needs to *see* the pictures. It must be *visual*.' She pointed to her eyes for emphasis.

'Do you have anything I can use? A template or something? Only I'm not very good at—'

'You'll have to make your own.'

I drew the shoes, school bag, lunch bag and coat myself. Everyone laughed. Stuart said the shoes look like the ones that the Mr Men wear and after about five days Tom developed an inability to focus on the uninteresting timetable.

*

I'm making the packed lunches in the kitchen when Stuart's mother, Maureen, phones. Her call suggests that Stuart spoke to her last night while I was on sentry duty outside Tom's bedroom. I fill her silences as I fill the children's sandwiches, occasionally excusing the *nee-naw* of Tom's fire engine and Letty's complaints about his volume. Maureen is the only person I know who can give the silent treatment over the telephone. Her calls are littered with enormous pauses. 'It's very noisy in your house this morning. I'm glad I'm not there,' she jokes before she hangs up.

'Me too,' I say into the silence of the dead line.

I fasten the lunch bags and carry them to the door. It's harder to forget things if you have to step over them on the way out. When it's time to go I call Tom and Letty. Letty lolls down the corridor, collecting her bag and coat on her way.

'Tom,' I shout up the stairs. 'Tom Parsons!' He ambles down, tieless. 'You'll have to go without your tie,' I tell him, even though this is as much a mark of failure as arriving late. 'And if you don't remember where you put your school bag right now, you'll have to go without that too.'

He disappears into the dining room and emerges with his bag. 'Under the table,' he explains.

I take it from him and open it. His tie is coiled in the bottom. I drag it out and he shows his teeth in a facsimile of a smile.

'I hate it when I don't have my tie,' he says as I unfold his collar and wrap the red strip around his neck.

The sky is clear as we drive to school. It will be a cold and sunny autumn day. Tom sits in the front, in case there's trouble.

'Look at the moon,' says Letty. 'I can still see it.' We all look up as we wait at the traffic lights. 'How far away do you think it is, Mummy?'

'Two hundred and thirty-eight thousand miles,' Tom says.

'Well, I think it's ninety-nine.' She smiles at me in the rear-view mirror.

'That's impossible. It would be far too close to the earth and there would be a big crash and everyone would be dead—'

'Except for Mummy.'

'I saw something about it in on TV and *everyone* died.'

'But not Mummy.'

'It was on TV, you idiot. Mum wasn't in it.'

'I can *imagine* that Mummy would be fine if—'

'You're STUPID!'

'STOP,' I shout as Tom's arm reaches to open the passenger door.

'He called me an idiot. And stupid.' Letty begins to cry.

'STOP,' I shout again as his hand wraps around the door handle.

'I don't want to sit here with YOU.'

'I haven't done anything,' I begin, forgetting my theoretical impartiality, my duty as referee.

'We don't want to sit here with you either, bozo,' Letty shouts.

I turn the CD player on. Nat King Cole is singing 'Smile' and Tom starts to sing too. He knows all the words. When he was small I took hundreds of photographs of him. He used to pucker and twist and screw his face into happiness. From behind the camera I sang. *Light up your face with gladness, hide every trace of sadness.* And he gurned, knitted and pleated himself into ugly knots. I thought he was being funny. I know all the words and Letty joins in with the chorus. If people could see us right now, they would be certain of our happiness.

We are not late. Letty prints sloppy, open-mouthed kisses on my face. I peel her off and deposit her outside the Reception Class entrance. I ruffle Tom's hair as he enters Class 2, which is as much as he allows. I see him taking off his coat. He isn't wearing his jumper. He must have left it at home. I watch him stand next to a girl he likes. He attempts a replica smile. The girl moves away and I witness his loneliness. His naked arms droop out of his short-sleeved shirt. If I fetch his jumper, at least he won't be cold. I poke my head around the door and ask his teacher about the sign.

'Just tell them they've got to take it down,' Stuart

said last night as he bundled his shirt into the washing machine. 'He'll be able to read those words before long. We don't want that, do we? Maybe you'll have got him sorted by then.'

'The sign is there for *information*,' the teacher insists. 'In case there's a supply teacher.'

I nod and smile and suggest that it's kept in the register. 'Sometimes people have to cover *at short notice* and the information needs to be *on hand* and *visible*.'

I keep smiling. I mention that the language of the sign could be seen as anti-inclusive by an inspection team and the teacher takes it down and throws it in the bin.

When I get home the house feels calm, as if I have caught it in the aftermath of a sigh. I load up the washing machine then drive back to school with Tom's jumper.

Home again, and I sweep the floors, make the beds and drink frothy coffee. In the lounge several of Tom's cars are guarding the perimeter of the dolls' house. Each one is a type of emergency vehicle. There are ambulances, fire engines, police Land Rovers and tow trucks. I am admiring the pleasing array of red, white and blue when the telephone rings.

'Did you get to school on time?' Maureen asks. 'I was worried.'

'Yes. Yes we did. Right on time. No problems.'

'Good,' she says. 'Good. That's something then.'

'Yes.'

'And what are you doing today?'

'Ironing, tidying up, cleaning.' I don't tell her about Tom's jumper. It will worry her. She will say that disorganisation is bound to *encourage* him. 'I'd better go if I'm going to get it all done before the kids—'

'There's an article in the *Daily Mail*,' she interrupts. 'About Asperger Syndrome.'

'Oh.'

'When I called before it sounded a bit hectic, and now I'm not sure whether to tell you. When I spoke to Stuart last night, he said you were upset. Said you had a funny five minutes. All better now?'

'Yes. I was just feeling sad because—'

'I read it this morning. Children who watch too much television. That's what it says. Too much television. I'm not saying that it applies to *you*, love. I want you to know that because I appreciate that you try very hard with him. But I was thinking that when he was small . . .' She thinks about this often: food additives, vaccinations, pesticides, lack of affection, attachment disorder, parenting classes, good old-fashioned discipline and gluten-free bread.

'I don't think . . .' I search for some polite words in the blockage that is piling up my throat. 'They both watch some television, but I really don't think . . . He didn't watch any more television than Letty and she's fine.' I carry the telephone to the kitchen and begin to make more coffee.

'Well, that's what it says here. I thought you could look it up on your computer.'

'Thank you.'

'I'm only trying to be helpful. I'm not saying that you . . . you know.'

'I know.'

'I wouldn't want you to think that I'm *having a go* or anything. I know you do your best.'

'Thank you.'

'And . . .'

'Yes?' I throw myself into the silence, unwilling to hear it expand into a suggestion of upset.

'I'm only saying this because I'm trying to help . . .'

'Yes?'

'Last time I came round there were cars all over the floor.'

'I know. Tom—'

'I'm not exaggerating for effect. They really were everywhere, all over the place. Now when Stuart was small I used to say to him, "Put that toy away before you get another one out," which kept everything tidy.'

'I know, but he—'

'Tidy home, tidy head. That's what my mother used to say. You can't have things straight in your mind if you're surrounded by a jumble.'

'I think it might make him happy. To get them all out. Arrange them,' I explain. Tom is always quiet as he orders the cars. Focused, contented, I like to imagine. The folds of his face flatten, and he is suddenly ordinary.

'He'll keep doing it if you let him get away with it.'

The coffee burns my lip as it creeps under the froth.

'Make sure you look that article up,' she reminds, as she concludes. *Tidy home, tidy head.* Speak to you soon, love.'

Before I collect the children, I put Tom's cars away. They make a satisfying crash as they land in the toy box. I find the wooden boy and girl upstairs in the nursery of the dolls' house with the miniature train and rocking horse. Wooden Dad is still on the sofa. The Dalek has moved. He's lying in the master bed under a pile of blankets. I can't find wooden Mum. She isn't in the dolls' house. I crawl across the lounge to check the toy boxes. She isn't with the train set, or the Bob the Builder toys. I check Letty's wooden farm. Wooden Mum isn't in the paddock or the barn. I open the hay loft and there she is, lying next to a little pig, her wooden face split by the red biro grin.

Letty's pencil case is poking out from underneath the sofa and it only takes a moment for me to find the red biro. I score its hard tip into the wood and drag wooden Mum's smile into an undulating frown. I sit on the floor holding the vandalised doll. I can see the autumn sky out of the lounge window. It reminds me of the day Tom was born. Afterwards, Stuart stroked my hair and said things like *good girl, well done, I love you so much.* Happiness penetrated my pethidine-fogged mind. It ballooned into the empty nest of my stomach and crept down my legs, reacquainting me with my feet. I was too happy to smile. I couldn't risk the joy escaping through my mouth like a puncture. From my hospital bed I could see a window which framed only sky. It was autumn blue, streaked with the white streamer-wisps of aeroplane contrails, as wide, and deep, and high as my elation. Stuart stroked me with gentle, trembling fingers and Tom dozed in the cot beside us. *I am the happiest woman in the world*, I thought.

Dancing in the kitchen

She is sewing pips of reminiscence in his fertile mind, selecting scenes for the reel of his memories. She is the Director, Writer and Make-up Artist. She would like to be the Film Editor too and supervise the relegation of her inadequacies to the cutting-room floor. She would like to censor any shameful language: 'You stupid boy,' 'I can't take you anywhere,' 'I should have thought twice about having children.' She does this in her Director's Cut. In this version she is always smiling. She makes delicious, nutritious meals, irons his favourite clothes in time for him to wear them, patiently explains homework and never shushes him in the car because she is listening to the radio. But she does not have final-cut privilege. He is The Editor of this portion of her life. He selects rare, single-take footage of her shouting and crying. He creates miserable montages of her mothering misdemeanours. 'Remember when I *really* wanted to go on a donkey and you wouldn't let me?' he asks. 'Remember when you said I would have to sleep in the loft with the wasps' nest if I kept getting out of bed?' he enquires.

She is determined to expunge her failings. She selects a location, prepares the storyboard and applies make-up.

Take One: Dancing in the Kitchen:

The radio is loud. The dance is a comedy combination of moves she used to perform in earnest several years ago. The noise will draw him to her and her exuberance will proclaim: I'm so happy to be your mother that I'm dancing in the kitchen. I love you so much, let's dance in the kitchen, together.

Take Two: Dancing in the Kitchen:

The radio is louder. This time he will forsake the television in order to investigate. He will burst into the kitchen and join in the dance. They will laugh together in a way that allows her to begin sentences with, 'Remember when we danced in the kitchen?'

Take Three: Dancing in the Kitchen:

The radio is moderately loud so as not to irritate him. He will come into the kitchen eventually, when he wants a drink or to ask what's for tea. He will chuckle at her dance.

Director's Cut: In the Kitchen:

The radio is on. Eventually he comes in. She sends him *such* a smile. Perhaps he will remember it.

Scaling never

There are so many kinds of never. There's the never that Jacob's mum uses when she says, 'Never talk to strangers, it's dangerous,' and there's the never his dad uses when he says, 'Never play with your food, it's bad manners.' But Mum talks to loads of people she doesn't know, and Dad breaks Oreos in half to lick the creamy bit. Issy used to say, 'I'll never be friends with you again if you don't play with me.' But she didn't mean it. And sometimes she said, 'I'll never eat sprouts.' She did mean this, and if Mum is right, and death is definitely the end of being alive, Issy will absolutely *never* eat sprouts. However, Jacob has noticed something. Never is a word that doesn't always mean not-on-your-nelly and absolutely no way. Sometimes never means not yet.

The house is full of sadness. It's packed into every crevice and corner like snow. There are bottomless drifts of it beside Issy's Cinderella beanbag in the lounge. The sadness gives Jacob the shivers and he takes refuge in the garden. Like the house, it is higgledy and unkempt. The lawn is scuffed and threadbare in places like a grassy doormat that's felt too many feet. It is speckled with fallen leaves. Overgrown flower beds stream along the length of each of the old, red brick garden walls, all the way to the end wall which is partially concealed by a hornbeam hedge. Randomly planted apple trees poke out of the lawn like twisted, witchy hands. Clusters of green fruit cling to bent branches which are already almost bare of leaves. Windfalls pepper the grass and Jacob kicks them as he makes his way to the end of the garden. Some of the fallen apples are rotten and they detonate, spraying pulp and larvae. Others are hard and thwack on contact like tennis balls.

Last year, Mum supervised an apple-picking operation before the trees dropped their fruit. There were bags and bags full. Mum took lots of the bags to church. Dad made an announcement in sacrament meeting that anyone who wanted a bag of apples could come and get one from the car boot afterwards. Lots of people wanted free apples and Mum smiled at all of them and said, 'You're welcome,' a lot. She wrapped the apples that she didn't give away in newspaper and put them in empty shoe boxes in the cupboard under the stairs. When she opened up the boxes several months later, the apples were pink and yellow, and soft. 'I had no idea this would happen,' she kept saying, as if it was the most incredible thing she'd ever seen. She made everyone come and look. It *was* a surprise that the apples weren't Brussel-sprout green and sour any more, but Mum said it was miraculous.

This year, she hasn't bothered. No one has bothered. Even the trees themselves seem to be fed up of balancing fruit in their knobbly branches and there are so many fallen apples to kick that it takes Jacob a long time to reach the end of the garden. When he gets there he stares at the hedge which is covered in crispy leaves that look like giant bran flakes. A few of them have fallen off, but he knows that most of them will cling on throughout the rest of the autumn and into the winter. He knows this because last winter he and Issy played unseen in the gap between the hedge and the wall, hidden from view by the screen of lingering leaves.

It was Issy who found the dead bird. Most of it was under the hedge, but one of its wings lay on the lawn, spread out in a feathery fan. It had probably been killed by next door's cat. Issy picked the wing up. Jacob opened his mouth but then closed his lips over the words he had been about to say: 'Put it down, it's unhygienic' was a sentence that belonged to Dad. Besides, he was suddenly keen to touch the wing himself. The feathers were shiny blue-black, and he had to know if they were both as sharp and as soft as they looked. Issy let him hold the wing, and he touched the feathers with his eyes closed. They were soft and fluffy at the tips and coarse and strong at the base where the shafts were thicker.

They buried the bird and its wing behind the hedge. They dug a hole with two plastic, seaside spades from the garden shed. Jacob placed the bird in the hole. One of its black eyes stared blankly at the sky.

'Don't put soil in the birdie's eye,' Issy said.

'We have to do it properly,' Jacob replied. Although it was the first burial he had ever attended, he was pretty certain that it wouldn't count if he left part of the bird peeping out from under the soil.

'Why don't you say a prayer?' he suggested.

Issy prayed. She said the prayer that they all said at every meal time, saying 'bird' instead of 'food'. She said it quickly, like they did when they were hungry and didn't want to wait any longer for their food.

'DearHeavenlyFather. Thank you for the bird. Please bless it. InthenameofJesusChrist. Amen.'

Jacob covered the bird with soil which he patted down with the back of his spade. They stood in the gap between the wall and the hedge for a few moments, flanked by dark red brick and brittle, hornbeam leaves.

'I think we should sing a song,' Issy said.

'Okay,' he replied. 'What song?'

'One about birdies.'

'Okay.' He tried to think of a song about birds. 'I think "In the Leafy Treetops" has some birds in it.'

'No.' Issy smoothed the bird's grave with the tip of her trainer. 'Something good.'

'I don't know.' He shrugged. He'd had enough. He was ready to do something else.

Then Issy started to sing:

'We will find a little nest in the branches of a tree.
Let us count the eggs inside; there are one, two, three.
Mother bird sits on the nest to hatch the eggs all three.
Father bird flies round and round to guard his family.'

Jacob gave her a brief round of applause.

'Do you think that it was a mummy birdie or a daddy birdie?' Issy asked, as they pushed themselves out from behind the hedge and onto the lawn.

'Dunno,' he said. 'We could have checked for a willy, but it's too late now. Maybe it was a child bird.'

'Oh.' Issy looked surprised. 'That *would* be sad.'

Jacob thinks he can remember the spot where they buried the bird. At first he isn't sure if he will do anything. He stands next to the hedge, daring himself. Then he dashes back to the shed quickly, as if he is worried that something might stop him.

Spade in hand, he pushes through the hard and scratchy criss-cross weave of branches and into the space between the wall and the hedge. He starts to dig. Nothing at first. He moves along a bit, his elbow grazing the wall. He disturbs more soil and he can suddenly smell clay and damp and he stops digging for a moment as he remembers.

*

He didn't want to go to the funeral. Mum was very upset when he said this. How could he not want to go to his sister's funeral – how *could* he? As he had expected, the funeral was just more church, different from Sundays only in that they had to sit on the front row, except for Dad who sat up on the stand as usual so that he could do the service. There was an opening and a closing prayer, there were some hymns and Dad did a talk about not being sad while tears coursed down Mum's face and sprinkled into her lap, watering her hands. Afterwards everyone drove to the cemetery. There was a very deep hole in the ground. When Jacob asked about it later, Dad said it had been dug by a mechanical digger. Someone had placed a fake grass carpet over the pile of earth that had been dug up, and Jacob stood on a corner of it, scratching the soles of his shoes along its prickles.

Dad and some of the funeral men carried the coffin from the car to the graveside. When they put it down on two planks of wood that had been placed over the hole, Mum started to make a noise. Dad moved away from the coffin and went to stand next to her. He put his arm around her shoulder, but the noise continued. It was a bit like a dog howling and it sent a zigzag of fear from Jacob's heart to his willy. A squirt of wee leaked into his pants and spread in a warm circle. Dad shushed Mum, but she wouldn't stop it, so he fished in his suit pocket and pulled out a handkerchief. He put it in Mum's hand. She just stood there, so he lifted her hand and held it over her mouth for her. The handkerchief muffled the noise. Eventually Dad let go and Mum carried on holding the handkerchief over her mouth, but the noise leaked past its edges.

Dad had to say a prayer to dedicate the grave. He said it loudly so people could hear him over Mum. It went on for a while, and Jacob wished that he would hurry up. After Dad finally finished, the funeral men made the coffin go down. When someone walked up and threw a handful of soil into the hole, Mum stopped making the noise. She moved the handkerchief away from her mouth.

'*Don't* do that,' she said.

People left quickly. Dad said Mum should say goodbye to everyone. Jacob heard her saying that she didn't see why she should, as she was going to see them all again in a few minutes for the food, back at the chapel. But she walked with Dad toward the parked cars anyway.

Jacob moved off the plastic grass and onto the real stuff. He edged toward the hole. Issy's coffin was a long way down and it was spattered with dirt. He knelt at the lip of the grave. The earth was damp, and he could feel wet soaking into the knees of his best trousers. He had been hoping for a miracle. Sister Anderson was always going on about them on Sundays in Primary lessons. Some miracles happened a long time ago, like Noah's Ark.

Not many people seem to have thought about it, but once when he couldn't sleep, Jacob had imagined how much poo the animals must have made, and how much trouble it must have been for Noah to stop them all from eating each other. It had made him realise that Noah's Ark was an ace miracle, right up there with Father Christmas's flying sleigh. There were other good miracles from the olden days, like The Feeding of the Five Thousand, Daniel in the Lion's Den and Balaam and the Talking Ass – a miracle with a rude word in it. Dad said that miracles happened all the time. Sister Anderson thought so too. She said that Brother Anderson's cancer treatment was proving to be a modern-day miracle. Maybe she was right, but Brother Anderson's head looked like an enormous egg, and Jacob had been imagining a much bigger miracle than that for Issy, one which would see her alive, and with hair. His tummy hurt. His underpants and knees were wet and cold, and a damp, sticky smell was wafting out of the hole in the ground. It reminded him of the bag of modelling clay that Mrs Slade kept on the side, next to the sink, in the school classroom. He looked at the soil speckles on the coffin's little silver plaque. It read, Isabel Rachael Bradley. He couldn't understand why anyone would want to throw dirt on Issy.

Sister Anderson crouched down next to him. 'It's very sad, isn't it?' she said.

'It was meningitis,' he told her.

Mum had made him say the word again and again.

'People will ask, so you must learn how to say it,' she said.

He practised it until it stopped sounding like a sticky eye infection – mengy-eye-tus, and started to sound more like men-ingiantis; a band of giants who had magicked Issy into the Celestial Kingdom.

'Are you all right, sweetheart?' Sister Anderson asked.

He wanted to say that he was fine. He wanted to tell her to go away. But his bottom lip began to wobble and it wouldn't stop, even when he bit it quite hard. Sister Anderson helped him to his feet. She put her arms around him and pulled his face into her squashy tummy. Her dress was pink and velvety. His tears soaked into its softness. She patted his head gently and said, 'It's such a shame.'

When he had finished crying he stepped away from her. A rope of snot stretched from his nose to the front of her dress, like a bridge.

Jacob unearths a feather and knows that he is in the right spot. The feather is matted and patchy, which is disappointing, but he keeps digging. As he digs he thinks about the apples, hiding in old shoe boxes in the cupboard under the stairs. He knows that like the apples, the bird will look different when it is uncovered and he hopes the transformation will be a good one.

There are more feathers, though most of them are not very feathery any more. He digs especially carefully now. He has seen an enormous book on Egypt in the school library. There is a section about digging stuff up. There are pictures of the tiny brushes people use so as not to damage anything. The corner of his spade grazes something hard. Jacob puts it down and begins to move the soil away with his fingers. Here is the bird's back. He follows its knobbles, brushing the dirt away. The bird is mostly bones. This is not the transformation he has been hoping for. The bird's insides, and most of its outsides, have melted into the soil. Its skeleton is a browny-grey colour. It's hard, but brittle, like crisps. He wipes soil from the bird's wing-twigs which, stripped of feathers, look like dirty icicles. Lastly, he moves the soil away from the bird's skull. The eye has gone. In its place is a hole which seems far too big. His finger may even fit inside. It does.

Mum used to read a fairy tale each night from the old, fat book that she had been given as a present when she was a little girl. Afterwards she would get the Bible and the Book of Mormon picture books out and read a story from one of them, too. Jacob's favourite fairy tale used to be 'The Wolf and the Seven Goats'. The best bit was the part where the mother goat opened up the wolf and her kids tumbled out of his big furry belly. 'The Wolf and the Seven Goats' is just made up. But the story of Jonah and the Whale actually happened in real life. Jonah got stuck in a whale and survived. In the Bible and the Book of Mormon there are even better stories than Jonah's. There are stories about people who died and then came back to life, like the story of Lazarus. Jacob remembers it because there's a bit where Lazarus is *so* dead that Martha says, 'He stinketh.' After they read about Lazarus, Mum occasionally said, 'Who stinketh?' when someone did a trump. There's the story of Jairus's daughter, too. Everyone thought she was dead, and people were crying. But Jesus told Jairus to believe, and when they reached the house, the girl wasn't dead any more. She was just sleeping. With God all things are possible – that's what it says on the picture of a big bird with its wings spread wide in flight on the kitchen wall.

After the funeral, Jacob asked Dad why he hadn't resurrected Issy. Dad said that priesthood holders can't just go around resurrecting everyone. He said that Heavenly Father decides if people live or die. Jacob replied that it wasn't always like that. Sometimes people *believe* and then miracles happen. Dad said it was true, but not in Issy's case. He said, 'Ours is not to question why.' He said that sometimes believing things will turn out all right in the end is a better kind of faith than the faith that raises people from the dead.

Jacob felt cross. 'So it's *all right in the end* for Issy to be dead?' he asked. 'Didn't you even try to make a miracle happen? What's the point of being in charge at church if you can't do miracles?'

Dad said that Jacob would understand it better when he got older. But Jacob understood something right then. If he wanted Issy back, he was going to have to make it happen himself.

The bird's eye socket rings the tip of Jacob's finger. He has been praying for the bird to come back to life for a whole week. It seemed sensible to start with something little, with a small miracle, for practice.

Sister Anderson once said that faith can be as small as a seed. She brought some mustard seeds to Primary for everyone to see. They were tiny. Jacob knows that his faith is bigger than a mustard seed; it's at least as big as a toffee bonbon, maybe bigger.

He moves his finger out of the bird's eye socket and picks up the spade. Then he puts it down. If he reburies the bird, he will have to dig it up and, if nothing has happened, rebury it again. He will have to keep checking on it. As the autumn sets into winter there will be days when it is raining and days when the ground is stiff with frost. It will be much easier if he can find a safe place to put the bird.

He pushes his fingers into the soil on either side of the bird's chest and lifts gently. The head is the first thing to fall off, followed by the wing that the cat didn't damage.

He is left holding a little cage of ribs, and as he places a finger under the spindly, dangling legs, they break off too. He thinks he might cry as a rush of salty prickles gather at the top of his nose, but he doesn't. He puts the ribs down and pulls the bottom of his T-shirt out with one hand. Then he picks the little pieces of bird up, one at a time, and drops them into his makeshift pocket. He bends to sniff the soily bones. They smell of earth. They definitely don't stinketh.

He doesn't kick any apples on his way back up the garden. If he is lucky, he will get up to his room without being noticed. Dad is at a church meeting. It's Mum he needs to watch out for. On Saturdays she usually cleans. According to the song they sing in Primary, Saturday is the day to get ready for Sunday. Mum always says that Sundays are easier to face with a clean house. But today she might just be sitting at the table in the kitchen, wet-faced and dribbly-nosed, staring at nothing.

The back door is half wood and half glass. Jacob approaches stealthily, ready to duck if necessary, but the kitchen is empty. He opens the door then sneaks along the linoleum. He tiptoes down the hall and turns to climb the stairs. He is half way up when he hears the toilet flush. He has to pass the bathroom door to reach his bedroom. He starts to run. The bird pieces jiggle in his T-shirt. He hears the rush of the taps and the clink of the towel ring as Mum dries her hands. He is quick. His door closes as the bathroom door opens, and he listens to his mum pad slowly down the stairs as he kneels on the carpet, behind the door, his heart jumping.

He isn't sure where to put the bird. Mum will be certain to find it if he puts it in the wardrobe. He could put it in the bottom of Issy's toy box, but he doesn't want to touch her stuff because it gives him tummy ache. He shuffles across the carpet on his knees until he reaches the bunk bed. He puts the bird pieces on the floor and then lies down on his tummy and commando-crawls under the bottom bunk. There is dust along the skirting boards like the grey fluff that collects in the tumble drier. Under the bed, he discovers a couple of plastic soldiers who have deserted and one of Issy's books that must have slipped down the side of her bunk. He moves the book and the soldiers out from under the bed, and then he carefully delivers the bird bits into the far corner underneath.

After he crawls out from under the bed, he kneels again. He folds his arms, bows his head and says a prayer.

'Dear Heavenly Father. I have faith that you can resurrect the bird. This is a real prayer. It's not like asking for a bike or something. It's very important. When you resurrect the bird, I will have even more faith. And then there can be even better miracles. In the name of Jesus Christ, Amen.'

As he gets to his feet, there's a knock at the door. Mum's head appears followed by her body and the Hoover.

'It's Saturday,' she says as she moves one of the toy boxes with her foot, in search of the wall plug. *The day we get ready for Sunday.*' She sings part of the Primary song to him with a half smile, as if she is hoping that he will join in. He doesn't. He picks the soldiers and Issy's book off the floor, climbs the ladder to his bunk, and waits for the scream of the Hoover. But Mum pauses for a moment.

'Would you . . . do you think we should . . . Are Issy's things *bothering* you?'

'Not really,' he fibs, his tummy clenching as he stares down at the orphaned jumble of Duplo, dolls and ponies with bright nylon hair. If he tells her the truth, she might throw them all away, and then Issy won't have anything to play with when she comes back.

Mum's voice jellies around her words as she says, 'We could sort them out, if you like.'

'Don't cry,' he says quickly.

'I wasn't . . .' She wipes a hand over her face, as if to make sure.

'Good. Leave Issy's things. It's okay. She might want them back—'

'Jacob, I've told you that we won't see her again until—'

'After she's resurrected, she might want them back,' he explains cunningly. 'Everyone gets resurrected at the end of the world. Dad said so.'

Mum lets out a big puff of air. 'That's a long way off.'

'You never know,' he says in a grown-up voice.

She smiles at his imitation of her and switches the Hoover on. He watches as she pushes it back and forth, mowing the carpet. She unclips the wiggler attachment and worms it into the gap between the toy boxes. It sucks along the skirting board, uncurling and stretching like an elephant's trunk.

Then she kneels down. And Jacob suddenly feels marooned on the top deck of the bunk, the captain of a vessel that is rapidly approaching Niagara Falls.

'Haven't you finished?' His question pierces the Hoover's greedy moan like a rescue shout.

'I'm just going to do under the bed,' she calls up to him. 'Goodness knows when I last did it.' She kneels on the floor and thrusts the wiggler about as if she is trying to capsize him.

'You don't have to do it today,' he exclaims, his thoughts paddling against the current of her decision like frantic hands.

There's a sound like the clatter of homemade shakers filled with uncooked rice and pasta, and his stomach sways as the bird bones rattle up the wiggler. He wants to launch himself off the top bunk and bodyslam the Hoover like a professional wrestler, but he sits still as it sucks up his hope.

'Have you got some Lego under here?' Mum starts to lie down on the floor to get a proper look under the bed.

'No,' he shouts down to her. 'I think it must be some . . . rubbish.'

She gets up and switches the Hoover off.

'I'll check for Lego when I empty it later, just to make sure.' She clips the wiggler back in place, unplugs the cord, and closes the door on her way out.

Jacob stays on his bunk for a bit, looking down at the room. Mum will probably forget to check the Hoover, which means he's not likely to get into trouble. That's good, it's something to feel happy about. He tries to feel happy. He pushes his cheeks up with his fingers and lifts his face into a smile, but his mouth pops open and a small sob spills out. He is disappointed to find himself so far from happy. He pulls back the duvet, lies down on his tummy and buries his head in the pillow. A series of sobs shake out of him and rattle into the pillow, grazing the back of his throat like tiny bones.

Eventually, he climbs down the ladder. With God, all things are possible. God helps those who help themselves and He loves a trier: if at first you don't succeed, try, try, try again. Remembering all this about God makes Jacob feel ever so slightly better. He puts the stray soldiers in his toy box, but he keeps hold of the book that was under the bed. It's the story of 'Jack and the Beanstalk'. He opens it to the middle page, which is a special, fold-out picture of the beanstalk, its tip is hidden by clouds. He knows that 'Jack and the Beanstalk' is not a miracle. It's just a fairy tale. No one could get some magic beans. It could *never* happen, not on your nelly, absolutely no way. Fairy tale nevers are not the kind of nevers that Jacob is looking for. He is in search of nevers that can be slipped under, scaled, or tiptoed around. But even though he knows that fairy tale nevers are impossible to bend, he wishes he had a beanstalk. He wishes that Sister Anderson would bring magic beans to Primary instead of mustard seeds. He wishes he could plant the magic beans at the bottom of the garden, behind the hedge, and watch an enormous stalk twist and stretch skyward. And even though Dad says that heaven is not actually in the sky, he wishes he could climb the stalk right up into the clouds and find Issy. That would be ace.

The baby aisle

The trolley was bursting and it was almost time to pick the twins up from nursery when the rhythmic mewling of newborns and a whiff of their fresh-out-of-the-belly smell encouraged her to have a quick peep down the baby aisle. She dug the disregarded shopping list out of her pocket and placed it on the trolley's vacant child seat for protection, a reminder of her resolution not to buy anything. The lamb-like wails of discontented infants washed into her ears on a wave of nostalgia. The sound seemed to interfere with the transmission of memory, allowing only the selected Hallmark highlights of motherhood to play in her mind. It reminded her of when the twins were tiny. It was the January sales two years ago when she pushed them through the checkout for the first time. They were an impulse buy. A BOGOF offer she couldn't resist. She wasn't the only one. There are several sets of non-identical twins at the nursery. Her own: Grace and Thomas, and another set from Tesco: Daniel and Georgia, along with Niklas and Salina from Lidl, and Kian and Keira from Kwik Save, before it went bust.

She bought her eldest, Samuel, six years ago. She and Peter argued about whether to get a boy or a girl. She gave in since Peter was so adamant. He chose a Samuel because it said 'active' on the box. He had big ideas about playing football in the park. When Samuel was two she popped to the shops to escape toilet training and tantrums, and returned with an irresistible Chloe. After that she hadn't planned on having any more, but when the twins were on offer two years ago it just happened. She entered the supermarket without the protection of a list, and the next thing she knew she was pushing a double-seated trolley.

Now she arms herself on visits to the supermarket. The list is holstered in the front pocket of her jeans, ready to be drawn, ready to avert disaster should she need it. And yet recently it hasn't offered the protection she has come to expect. Occasionally she loses focus, lets her guard down. Away from the burnt toast smell, the crumbs and the discarded pyjamas of morning, there are possibilities, choices which seem entirely her own.

Today she started at the front of the shop. She sash-ayed past the books, wrapping paper and cards. Streamed a zigzag down the non-food aisles, glancing at televisions, kitchen implements, photograph albums and furniture. When she'd browsed the mobile phones, the smell of bread pulled her to the bakery. In between racks of freshly wrapped, perspiring loaves she glimpsed the staff sliding trays of buns into industrial ovens. A crate of fresh, cheesy bread was waiting to be placed on a wire shelf. It was floppy and warm. The smell went straight to her head. Despite her resolution to stick to the list, she put two batons in the trolley. And, in the face of her weakening resolve, she helped herself to a cinnamon roll, an almond croissant, and a box of caramel shortbread: *New and Improved*. She shopped at Waitrose once, but you couldn't help yourself there. The in-store bakery was old-fashioned. The cakes sat behind glass like sculptures and when she asked for *two* slices of white chocolate tiramisu, she felt like Oliver Twist. There were things in Waitrose that she had never seen before. Shellfish platters crammed with so many legs it seemed that they might scuttle away if she averted her eyes. Tians and terrines layered in fishy, eggy stripes. Posh pork pies topped with apricots and cranberries. Food that she couldn't pronounce: mini galettes, blinis and bright, rubbery-raw fish lined up in slimy, sparkling rectangles. She couldn't find the chicken nuggets and the baby aisle was packed with Archies, Sebastians and Theodores. She went back to Tesco the following week.

From the bakery she whizzed to the produce aisle and, in defiance of the arctic weather, grabbed a punnet of strawberries. An elderly man with a shopping basket smiled at her. 'Strawberries, eh?'

'Yes.' She smiled and nodded at him.

'What about cream?' The old man peered into her

trolley and laughed as if he had made a wonderful joke. 'You'd better get cream. Don't do anything by halves.'

'Yes.' She smiled again. This time the smile stretched, and she propped it up with her teeth.

'Any kiddies at home?' he asked.

'Yes.'

'Bet they like strawberries,' he said.

'Yes.'

'How many kiddies?'

'Four.'

'Four? Goodness me!' She waited for him to say *you don't look old enough*. But he didn't, confirming her fear that she was beginning to wear motherhood around her eyes and in the recently deepening parentheses bracketing her smile. 'Four!' He beamed at her again. 'How old?'

'Six, four and the twins are two,' she said.

'Twins!' He was delighted. He patted her shoulder in congratulation. 'Two for the price of one!'

'Yes,' she said.

In the cereal aisle, Frosties were on special offer. Two boxes for £2. She put a box of Weetabix in the trolley too, a rationalisation destined to sit in a kitchen cupboard with the others. In the next aisle she was drawn to the yellow sign under the Thornton's chocolates, *SAVE £1.50*. She saved £3.

When the trolley was bursting with bargains and she'd saved almost as much as she'd spent, it was time to pay, and it was at precisely that moment that the sound and the smell of the baby aisle beckoned. There was a sign at each end of the aisle: *You have peace of mind knowing that these children are maximum quality, organic and fair trade.* The aisle was packed with Olivias, Rubys and Jessicas. There were rows of Jacks, Harrys and Joshuas. Each child was tagged with an appropriately-coloured label. She stopped to examine a Lily. The Lily was virtually bald and her eyes were the murky, undecided, blue-black of newborns. There was information on her box. *Expected life span: up to 86 years (less if raised in Glasgow, may be considerably less in non-EU countries). Height: typically 157–177 cm. Weight: 50–80 kg. New 100-day quality guarantee – exclusions apply.*

She moved along the aisle slowly, past the fresh stock and into the Reduced to Clear section. These babies were nearing their best-before dates. They made angry eye contact and cried real tears. She suspected that some of them had been returned, and she shivered as she remembered trying to return Samuel while Peter was at work one day.

'What do you mean, you won't take him back?' she'd cried, dizzy with tiredness, her ears ringing with his relentless caterwauling.

'We only take them back if there's a fault,' the manager had said.

'But I've got my receipt.'

'Persistent crying is not a valid reason for return, I'm afraid. It's all in the small print on the underside of the box.' The manager began to recite it by heart, as if he went through this several times a day. 'The baby must be returned with all its accessories, packaging, instructions, et cetera, and must be in unused condition. All warranty claims must be made within thirty days. A proof of purchase must be supplied—'

'I said I have the—'

'You must return any free gift that came with the baby. We will not accept any baby that has been personalised . . .'

She turned away and stumbled out of the store with Samuel. It wasn't long before a little more sleep and a little less screaming made the experience bearable. Peter hadn't needed to know.

She poked around the Reduced to Clear section wondering if there was a bargain to be had. There was a half-price George with fanning ears and a Maya with red hair. The Maya was tempting. She picked her up and the baby smiled thick, empty gums at her.

A young man in a blue uniform approached. 'Can I help you?'

'No, thank you. I'm just looking.' She put the baby back.

'We have some great deals today,' he said, with a sweeping gesture that encompassed the Reduced to Clear infants. 'What exactly are you looking for?'

'Nothing,' she said, glancing at her list.

'Oh, a list.' He rolled his eyes. 'You don't need one of them. They ruin the mood.'

She opened her mouth to reply, but he beat her to it.

'It's no fun with a list and your list is much too small. I can tell. Anyway, lists don't work.' He picked the Maya up. 'Isn't she lovely?' he asked.

'Yes,' she replied. 'She is lovely, but I already have—'

'And I wouldn't call her ginger, would you? I'd say she's more of a strawberry blonde. Look, it says here: "Studious and teachable". She's reduced. Think of how much you'll save.'

The Maya began to cry. It was a rasping cry, pathetic and airy. Her hands extended and contracted as she sobbed, as if she was reaching.

'I'm sorry,' she said, itching to pick the baby up and console her, but determined not to do it in front of him. 'I already have four children. I really don't need any more.'

'But do you have a Maya?' he asked quickly. 'Brand new, latest model. Built to last longer than your others.'

She shook her head at him.

A tinny voice from above called, 'All till-trained staff report to checkouts immediately, please.'

The young man shrugged at her and began to walk toward the tills. As he reached the end of the aisle he turned and said, 'If you change your mind later, I can't guarantee that she'll still be here.'

When she got home she gobbled the almond croissant and the cinnamon roll as she unpacked the shopping.

She put the Weetabix in the top cupboard, and she hid the Thornton's chocolates under a 3-kilo family bag of pasta. She left the box of caramel shortbread in the car for the twins to nibble on the way home from nursery.

And afterwards, when Peter arrived home from work and they sat around the dining-room table as good families should, she stocked the conversation with improved attentiveness, and longer-lasting laughter, in order to conceal the hoarse, feeble cries emanating from a toy box in the lounge.

My burglar

He always comes at night. In the thick of dark. In the solid, black stillness. In the quiet. In the smothering, pitch silence that stifles the house. I hear the pattern of his feet in the wide hush that packs each room. I hear the snap and creak of the floorboards. The whisper of his hands on the banister. The tide of his breath. I smell the stale tang of urine, of sweat, of wide, yawning pores. I don't scream. There's no point. I'm alone. I sit up in bed and push my back to the headboard. I keep still. I peer into the inky darkness, searching for a partition of shadow and form.

Although he has left *me* alone, he has stolen my Accurist watch, an emerald necklace, a pen and my address book. I watch television. I know about burglars. A man from Birmingham said he was burgled twenty-three times last year. He claimed for twenty-three televisions and the insurance company was very angry about it. I saw it on the BBC. Burglars keep coming back.

I am beginning to suspect that my burglar is looking for something. I don't believe he is creeping about my house on the off-chance. I think he is after my locket.

'Don't be silly, Mum,' says my daughter Charlotte, on the telephone, bossy and officious. 'How on earth would anybody know about your locket?'

I wear it, don't I? How easy it would be for someone to catch a glimpse of it around my neck in the grocers,' or see it sparkle in the large-print section of the library. How straightforward it would be to wait with me at the bus stop, board with me, alight with me. How simple it would be to follow me down Topsham Road and watch me enter number forty. And how effortless to return later, in the dark, to search for the locket.

'You're being ridiculous, Mum,' says my daughter, Charlotte, on the telephone, unsympathetic and sceptical. 'You *lost* that set of keys, they've not been *stolen*. You keep saying you'll get the locks changed and you haven't. I'm going to have to look on the internet – send someone round to do it. There's no burglar.'

Charlotte lives in Ireland. She's been very rude recently.

Night doesn't fall in the late autumn, it plunges. It catches me unawares. It crashes around me, throwing itself through the house like an unstoppable, black breaker, and I chase after, switching on lights in its wake, until the whole house is shining like a warning flare. For all my burglar knows, I have guests, a party, family visiting. I feel like Cinderella, safe until the clock strikes twelve. No one of my age would be entertaining after twelve. I always turn the lights off and hurry to bed before midnight strikes. The only thing worse than hiding from him in the darkness would be confronting him in the full glare of light.

My television breaks the broad silence of evening. So many channels. Just enough time to make a cup of tea during the adverts, so long as you remember to switch on the kettle. I like programmes about Americans with obesity. They do these operations on them to stop them from eating. Sometimes they suck the fat out of them with a tube like a vacuum cleaner. Afterwards they all cry and hug each other. It's very entertaining.

Tonight I'm not watching television. Tonight I'm looking for a hiding place for my locket. My locket is silver. It's Victorian, oval-shaped. It belonged to my mother. It's such a long time since I took it off that it was extremely difficult to undo the clasp. But it's done. Here it hangs, in knotty fingers that I can hardly believe are my own. The locket is worth a lot of money.

'For God's sake, don't lose it, Mum,' says my daughter, Charlotte, on the telephone, impatient and brusque. 'You seem to be losing all sorts at the moment.'

I dare say Charlotte is looking forward to inheriting it.

It's no use hiding things under beds or in mattresses; they're the first places people look. Unexpected places are best. Sometimes I surprise myself with my ingenuity. Once I discovered my wedding ring in the bread bin. What a marvellous hiding place. Who would think to check there? The kitchen is a good place to hide things.

The locket dangles as I examine the worktop: breadbin, biscuit tin, kettle. I plop the locket into the kettle. He will never look there.

Midnight.

The chimes of the dining-room clock carry up the stairs. If there had been time I would have changed the bed. There is nothing like sliding into sheets that have been dried on the line, soaked in the season, fragrant and fresh. Perhaps tomorrow. The darkness presses me flat to the sheet. I breathe softly. I listen.

Morning.

Morning perforates the darkness. He has been. He has been and the stench of him fills the space where the darkness was. The sheet is moist. Perhaps it was still damp when I changed the bed last night. I clean the teeth that are mine, insert the teeth that aren't and stare into the bathroom mirror at the bloodshot eyes and furrowed face reflected there.

My locket.

I check the bed. Pull off the sheet. Perhaps it came off in the night. But no, the clasp was far too tight. Oh, the smell. He has been here, in my room while I slept. He has fumbled sweaty fingers around my neck, removed my locket and stolen it.

In the kitchen the water tinkles into the kettle. I watch it boil. I make tea and dial my daughter's number. Her name is Charlotte. She lives in Ireland.

The countdown

He kills the baby by accident.

He carries her in one arm, cradling her head between chest and bicep. His hand palms her tiny backside. He can feel her malleable skeleton under the slack of her grow-into-me skin as her legs shrimp toward her middle.

He braves the slate floor tiles one step at a time in the non-slip, sticky-soled socks he has begun to hoard. He concentrates on the careful pad of his feet, the stick and rip of the plastic knobbles as they find the floor. He leans over the deep, farmhouse sink to retrieve something from the windowsill: a bottle of antibacterial hand wash, a scouring pad. Then he drops her. She splinters into slivers of bone and rivulets of connective tissue. He hears his wife's footfall on the stairs. His wife is coming. His wife is coming and he can't jigsaw the fragments in the sink into anything that resembles a baby . . .

He indicates and pulls over. He peels gluey hands from the steering wheel, rubs them over his forehead and into the fuzz of his hair. It's worse when he kills her while driving because he can't do anything about it. When he's at home he checks the child-locked cupboard, matches its contents to the alphabetised list. But it's harder in the car.

He switches the radio on. The FM frequency runs from 87.7 Bailrigg FM to 107.9 Dune FM. He searches for the middle, like the Grand Old Duke of York, hunting for the line of symmetry that will leave him neither up, nor down. The centre of the frequency is 97.8 FM, Radio One, but he is too far from the Burnley and Colne Valley transmitter to hear past the crackle. He edges the dial to 98.9 to pick up the North West transmitter. Although 98.9 is not in the middle of the FM frequency, the eight is flanked by nines in a way that is quite reassuring. He turns the volume up to eighteen. He indicates and pulls back into the rush-hour traffic.

The radio raps a chorus advising him to *let it go*. He is safe, bubbled by the number eight. He has sliced himself right through the middle of its circles. But when the verse shouts, 'It don't make me happy to watch you suffer,' he topples back into imagination.

He kills the baby by accident.

He puts her to bed in the brand-new cot which conforms to BS EN716. The bars are the correct distance apart and the mattress fits snugly. There are no corner-post extensions and no decorative cut-outs in the headboard or footboard which could trap her limbs. The blinds and their dangling, strangulating cords have been replaced with curtains. He places a blanket over the fling of her sleepy limbs and whispers goodnight.

When he returns, the baby's room is bursting with held breath. The blanket conceals her so respectfully that he almost apologises as he lifts a fear-confirming corner. She is stock-still, flooded with violet and lilac. She has stalled, he tells himself. This is an adjournment, not an ending. He hears the bed creak in the next room as his wife gets up. He blows through the baby's cold lips, but the air puffs back at him. His wife is coming. His wife is coming and he can't breathe the baby back to life . . .

He indicates and pulls over. He switches the radio to Medium Wave. Medium Wave stretches from 198 to 1602, but he can only receive up to 1557 in the car, a spiky number and Radio Lancashire, besides. Radio Merseyside is almost in the middle of the frequency and the DJ's surname is Hoban, which is good because 'H' is the eighth letter of the alphabet. He pictures himself looped inside the lower circle of the number eight as he indicates and pulls back into the rush-hour traffic. The radio plays 'In my Life' as he approaches Switch Island. His mum loved this song. 'Who'd believe that John was only twenty-five when he wrote it,' she used to say.

Mum must have been about twenty-five when he began to count himself calm. One night he'd been chased out of sleep by a dream of a masked man in a dark cloak. He found his way to Mum's bed, but it was empty and there was something about the sound and feel of the air that told him he was alone in the house. He hid underneath Mum's duvet. His hot breath puffed into its thickness, dewing his face. Eventually he heard the soft click of the front door. When Mum climbed into bed she said she'd only been downstairs, but he didn't believe her. He was seven, not stupid.

The following night Mum came up to check on him at about nine o'clock. She smelt of perfume and he realised that she was going out again.

'I can't get to sleep,' he said.

'Try counting,' she'd replied. 'When I was little and I couldn't sleep, Nanna used to tell me to count sheep.'

A while later he heard the soft click of the front door. His ears hummed with the clank of pipes, the settling of the floorboards, his own heart beat and other sounds that he was perhaps imagining, although he couldn't be sure. The slither of a giant python as it wriggled up the stairs, the furry pitter-patter of eight enormous spider legs, the breezy blow of a ghost's robe. He began to count. He hurled numbers at his out-of-order imagination until the front door clicked again. It was the first time he'd counted past ten thousand.

He learned his times tables up to twelve before everyone else in his class and he was the only child to learn them up to fifty. He knew that it was sixty-three steps from the Year Two classroom to the school hall, and twenty-four steps to the boys' toilets. He made his mum move the wardrobe so it was exactly in the middle of the back wall of his bedroom which meant, he sensed, that monsters would not be able to climb out of it during the night. Mum joked that he was obsessed with numbers. She was wrong. Numbers weren't the problem, they were the antidote to his increasingly unmanageable imagination.

He exits the M57 at the first junction and the Radio Merseyside DJ starts to talk about the Liverpool game. 'If current form's anything to go by, we're gonna get hammered.'

He kills the baby by accident.

He places her in the bouncy chair. He fastens the safety belt around the crescent of her milk-filled belly. He sits on the sofa and watches as she frogs her legs and blinks her hands in response to the light and sound of the television. His slate Celtic Knot wall plaque, a criss-cross of five squares and twenty triangles, hangs on the wall above her. He used 6mm wall plugs when he hung the plaque. Perhaps he should have used the 8mm plugs. The doubt-trickle swamps him as the plaque begins its slide down the wall toward the baby's head.

There is a sound like the crack of an egg. A wet, zigzag split of skin and skull.

His wife calls, 'Would you like a cup of tea?' She calls again and then her footsteps follow the question. His wife is coming. His wife is coming and he can't uncover the command that will lift his legs from the sofa . . .

He indicates and pulls into his driveway. He finds neutral and lifts the handbrake up two notches. He swivels every dial and lever to either midway or twelve o'clock. He switches off the engine. He counts to eight, eight times. He counts up to sixty-four then down from sixty-four in an orbit of eights.

It's five fifty-nine. When it's six o'clock he will get out of the car. He will walk seven steps to the house and open the front door. He will wipe his feet four times. He will go straight to the lounge and remove the slate plaque from the wall. He will place it in the child-locked cupboard with the other hazardous objects that his imagination has identified. He will write *Celtic Knot wall plaque* between *candles* and *corkscrew* on the alphabetised list.

His wife will ask what he is doing. He will tell her that he has removed the plaque because he is hoping to paint the lounge. She will ask him to decorate the kitchen first because she wants to put the kettle and the knives back on the worktop. She will say that she can't understand why the apple corer, the frying pan and the potato peeler are in the cupboard. She will take a deep breath, gulp her irritation away and ask what she can do to make him feel better. She will ask if he would like her to disinfect the things that he has hidden in the cupboard.

He will close the distance between them. Will stand behind her and nudge his face into the hollow between her ear and the right angle of her jaw. He will smooth his hands over the hemisphere of her belly.

She will say, 'Not long to go now. I can't wait, can you?'

He will hum agreement into the warmth of her neck. And he will trace a finger pattern of assuring eights over the elastic stretch of skin that presently shelters their baby.

Bed rest

We're just pulling the curtains around so as not to frighten the other parents.

That's not what the nurse says. But it is what she means. What she actually says is, 'We're just pulling the curtains around for privacy.'

The curtains go *shush* as they horseshoe around, hiding us in a thick pocket. I stare at the curtains, rather than the incubator. They are criss-crossed with local landmarks in green and beige. They must have been made specially. It costs so much to watch television in hospital nowadays. In Exeter you can watch the curtains instead. I trace the fabric map of the city with gritty eyes: the Cricklepit Suspension Bridge, the cathedral, the clock tower and the river as it bends and curls around and in-between them all. Right at eye level is a picture of the hand-operated cable ferry that runs across the river about a mile away from my parents' house.

The summer I was seven it was hot, and the weeks spread out in a buttery stretch of yellow. Our small garden buzzed and twitched with thousands of wriggly, crawly things. What was left of the grass was brick-warm and dust crusted, and lying on it had me in big trouble with Dad for making more washing. The bright evenings were fraught with leg ache and sleeplessness, occasionally broken by the manic chimes of the ice-cream van.

'Stupid van,' Dad used to say. 'Waste of money. I'll kill him if he wakes your mother up.'

The ice-cream van came round during the day, too. It stopped almost directly outside our house, and all along Burnthouse Lane children burst out of front doors, like the rats in the Pied Piper. They swarmed around the van, pushing each other to be first. And when the ice-cream man drove away, they chased him off the estate. Emily and I used to watch from behind the garden gates. We weren't allowed to play out with the other children.

'I've got more than enough to worry about, without you two disappearing,' Dad said.

Sometimes children came and chatted to us through the bars of the gate. 'Why don't you just come out?' they said. 'Just open these up.'

But we didn't dare. We didn't want to make things worse. Neither Emily nor I mentioned Mum to anyone. We barely mentioned her to each other. The agreement to keep quiet was unspoken but nonetheless binding. Mum had been in bed all summer. She was having bed rest. There was talk of pre-eclampsia, pre-eclamsia, I thought at the time, and I imagined her stomach eventually opening like an enormous white shell to reveal the baby hiding under her stretched skin. She was confined to the master bedroom where she lay in a passive, swollen pile. We weren't allowed in the room unless Dad said so. When we did go in she would graft a smile on, but it was temporary and usually peeled away within minutes. It smelt bad in there. It occurred to me that Dad didn't like the smell either because he was sleeping on the sofa. I thought that he shared my disgust of her as she lay sweating on the bed, full of my brother. But I was wrong. Whenever I tried to ally myself with his repulsion he flattened me. 'What smell? What are you talking about? Don't be so rude.'

It seemed as if my brother was expanding into Mum's arms and legs, growing furiously in the heat like the ponderous, baby-headed sunflowers we'd planted in the early spring. Her lack of restraint was frightening. What if she grew and grew like the enormous turnip or the dog called Digby who was the biggest dog in the world?

'Don't be silly,' said Dad. 'It's natural, it's biology. Everything will get back to normal.'

Dad's high-school biology class might have found his confidence reassuring, but I didn't. Mum used to be small and neat. She was ugly spread out all over the place. And she just kept on growing.

While it was my prerogative to imagine the worst, it was Emily's to act as if it had already happened. 'Your sister is *sensitive*,' Dad would say, as if it was something wonderful.

Emily was delicate, easily hurt. She sucked up emotion like a vacuum cleaner. At times she was puffed with it. 'What's wrong?' we would ask. Sometimes she would share her sadness, but it was carefully rationed. 'What's the matter, darling? Come on, tell us,' Mum and Dad cajoled. They spent many enjoyable moments engaged in this form of alchemy, searching for the correct combination of reassurance and placation to heal Emily's wounds.

In the early days of bed rest, Emily and I used to sneak upstairs and crawl into bed with Mum. She listened to us chatter and sometimes read us stories. But as it got hotter, she grew fatter and more tired, and Dad said enough was enough and we weren't to bother her. Emily continued to sneak upstairs on her own. Sometimes Mum didn't mind and Emily would be gone for a while. Other times Mum rang the bell on her bedside table and Dad stomped upstairs to remove Emily. 'It's too hot,' he'd say to her. 'Mummy's uncomfortable and she's sore from the injections. You're five. A big girl now.'

The nurse came every day to inject iron. She was due to arrive on the day near the end of the holidays when Emily made a final attempt to invade Mum's rest. Dad was emptying the washing machine with seething irritation, dragging the tangled intestine twist of clothes into the basket. He lacked Mum's patience. He cooked the meals and vacuumed aggressively. He chuntered as he ironed, remonstrating with the creases. When Mum's bell rang, Dad huffed out of the kitchen and up the stairs. He returned with Emily in his arms and planted her on the floor next to the washing machine. Immobilised by hurt, she lingered like a little ghost. I gave her a push, then a pull, into the garden.

She wouldn't play explorers or collect brown-tipped rose petals to make perfume. She wouldn't come and look when I started turning over stones to check for beetles and woodlice. Even the frenzied chimes of the ice-cream van failed to elicit a response. She was stiff with misery. So when the ice-cream van pulled up, I snuck through the garden gate, crossed the road, and stood in the wriggling swarm of children. Eventually it was my turn.

'I'd like an ice cream, please,' I said.

'Do you have any money?'

I'd forgotten about that. 'No. But if you just wait here, I'll go and get some.' I ran back across the road, through the gate, past the catatonic Emily and into the kitchen, colliding with Dad who was on his way outside with the basket of washing. 'The ice-cream man's waiting.' I said. 'I told him to wait while I get some money. It's not for me, it's for—'

He dropped the washing basket. Maybe the blood rushed to my head as he lifted me in the air and flung me over his knee. Perhaps I was looking at the geometric pattern on the linoleum as he hit me. When I remember it though, I am standing next to Emily, my mouth a big O of surprise, watching myself flail and shout as the ice-cream van tinkles into the distance and Dad expels five weeks of bed-rest frustration on my backside.

Emily cheered up after that. The nurse came to give Mum her injection and after lunch Dad produced a doll that was probably meant to be a present from my baby brother when he eventually made his appearance. 'It's been a rotten holiday,' he said by way of apology as he handed the doll to me.

The doll was clearly a bribe, offered in exchange for my forgetfulness. But I was determined to exact revenge by remembering. Seven is old enough to bear a grudge. The doll had a soft body, and plastic hands and feet. Her head was also plastic and her hair poked out in waving, ash-blonde tufts. Her eyes opened when she was upright and closed when she was horizontal. She was wearing a pair of blue corduroy trousers and a knitted sweater.

'Let's go for a walk,' Dad said. 'Just down to the river.'

And that's the trip I remember as I stare at the cable ferry, suspended on the hospital curtain in front of me.

My baby is in the transparent incubator that already resembles a coffin. Apparently, it's for the best. It's just a matter of time, and it's no longer a case of if, but when. That explains the curtains: no dying in public, please.

Emily is murmuring into the incubator's half-open porthole. I can't hear what she's saying, and I'm glad. Andrew called her when I went into labour. I caught snatches of his *'Far too early,'* his *'What are we going to do?'* and his *'Please come,'* in between contractions.

As I scrutinise the curtains, Emily sits in what has become her chair. She has soaked up all the grief around us like a piece of blotting paper. If she jumped on the spot I bet I would hear it sloshing around inside her. Andrew is exhausted. He is napping in the parents' room. But I can't sleep. 'Just go and have a rest,' one of the nurses likes to say, and I nod until she leaves me alone.

We are tucked away on the top floor of the hospital. This ward hides at the end of a bare corridor like a terrible secret. Visitors need permission to step past the double doors, yet Mum and Dad *popped by* three times yesterday. They tried to make it sound like they happened to be passing.

'We've just come to say hello,' Dad said.

'James sends love to you and his little niece,' Mum added, as if my brother had phoned from university between every one of their visits in order to send another slice of his love.

When the doctors first brought my baby up from maternity last week, she was lying on her front. She was conscious and her shoulder blades stuck out like tiny wings. Her skin was baggy as if I'd purposefully made it too big for her to grow into. Her arms and legs were trans-lucent, spindling out of her prone body in capellini threads. She seemed ancient; a tiny, old woman covered in whorls of beardy hair. Now she is on her back. Floored by kidney failure. Every spare fold of wrinkly, baby skin has ballooned with fluid. She is pearly smooth, shining as she stretches. The respirator expands her pneumonic lungs with the steady thwack of a hiccough. Tubes tentacle everywhere. Emily talks to her. I can't say anything. Shameful thoughts have been creeping around my mind all morning. If I open my mouth they might erupt into words. Thoughts like this one: although it's written on her tags, I can't call her by *that* name. It wasn't meant for a baby like her; it's my favourite name, and now I'll never get to use it. Or this: I'm going to have to change banks. There's a cashier at my bank who was so friendly. *How long now, love?* I never want to see him again. And this: I've stopped touching her through the porthole in the side of the incubator. I'm scared of her.

While I was mooching around, swollen and smug, chatting to strangers about due dates and ultrasound scans, it was all about to go wrong and I didn't even know it. All that benevolence and self-satisfaction, basking in the outpouring of goodwill, watching myself in shop windows, entirely unprepared for the trick my body was about to play on me.

'We'll just whizz her up to special care,' they said after she was born. 'Help her breathe for a bit. Give you a rest.'

Special care, whizz . . . *Intensive Care, rush.*

'She's going to need a little bit of help.' *Shit, this baby's even smaller than we were expecting.*

'Nothing to worry about.' *We're very worried.*

'You can hold her in a minute.' *We're taking her away from you.*

There is no time or geography here. The air is warm and withering, thick with beeps, hisses and whispers. There's no window in our cordoned corner. Only the curtains hint at a world outside with air and sky and a cable ferry.

I carried the new doll with me as we walked by the river. The afternoon hummed with heat and insects. When we reached the pub opposite the cable-ferry crossing, Dad bought a pint and two small glasses of lemonade. We sat at a picnic table. Emily and I sipped our drinks through bendy straws and watched the ferry creep toward and then away from us across the width of the river.

I asked Dad if we could go on the ferry. In likely anticipation of bath time and the unprecedented sight of his finger-stamps blooming across my backside, he agreed. He gave Emily and me 10p each, enough for a return trip, and nodded and waved to the ferryman as we paid our fares.

The ferry had bench seats down the port and starboard sides. There weren't any seats in the middle, so the ferryman could pull the boat along the thick cable that was attached to a post on either side of the river. A rail tracked behind the seats, like the back of a chair, a nod to safety that seemed sufficient back then.

We waved to Dad on the outward trip. He sipped his pint and gave a salute. I lifted the as-yet nameless doll from the seat between us and waved her too. When we reached the far bank we were stationary for a couple of minutes while the ferryman helped people alight and collected money from new passengers. Emily and I swivelled around on our seats, kneeling on the warm, soft wood, resting our elbows and chins on the slender metal safety rail.

I have always thought that there are two types of imagination: hopeful and inoculating. Even as a child I tended to avoid the hopeful kind, as a way of dodging disappointment. I dispensed with happy daydreams out of the same superstition that causes people to sidestep ladders. I preferred to use my imagination for prevention rather than cure: a means of injecting myself with enough disappointment and terror to protect against a future epidemic. It seemed that imagining the worst might prevent it from ever happening. On that August afternoon the river was liquorice soup. As we leaned over the rail it occurred to me that it would be easy for Emily to slide under it, into the darkness. Within seconds it would be unclear where to dive, where to clutch and snatch. It would be like blind man's bluff. Emily would sink deeper and deeper, into the black, silty bottom of the river, tangling in the tightening reeds as she struggled. A flip of my stomach warned of an imaginative overdose. Too late. Emily's drowning face floated through my thoughts with impunity.

'What will you call the dolly?' Emily asked as the boat began its return trip.

'Not telling,' I managed, blinking the fabrication of her struggling, waterlogged features away.

'She has to have a name.'

Emily let go of the rail and reached for the doll on the seat between us. I grabbed it with one hand and seized Emily's arm with the other in an attempt to force her elbow back onto the rail. Emily wobbled. There was a splash.

'It's very sad.'

I don't realise that Emily is talking to me until she says it again, 'It's very sad.'

'I know.'

'It's the saddest thing I've ever seen.'

'Me too,' I say, as if I am a casual observer. As if I am watching the news or a documentary about neonatal care.

'*Very* sad.' She looks as if she might cry. If she cries she might leave. She might need to get tissues or a cup of tea from the canteen. And I will be alone.

'Look at the curtains,' I say.

'The *curtains?*'

'Look. They're like a map. See the cable ferry?'

She shakes her head at me.

'Remember that summer . . .' I stop talking as she stands.

'I'm going out for a bit,' she says.

'Don't—'

'I need to,' she says and swishes the curtains open. 'You should be sitting there.'

She points at the chair and then closes the curtains behind her. The empty chair gapes accusation at me, so I sit down. When we were small and we got tired and upset Mum used to say, 'You're beyond'. I'm beyond, pushed further than the limits of my imagination. I tried to vaccinate myself against something like this. As a teenager I read Dad's embryology text book. It was locked in the glass cabinet in the lounge next to *The Body Book* with its well-thumbed central pages: line drawings of a man and a woman jigsawed together in what seemed, back then at least, like a progression of intricate exercises. The embryology book was Dad's from university. He said it was in the cabinet because it was *upsetting*. I spent many immunising hours examining the magnitude of human deformity: a baby with his insides out, another with a nose in the middle of its forehead, fists without fingers, supplementary limbs, partially-formed genitals, and polycephaly. I thought it was enough. Prematurity and multiple organ failure weren't in the book.

She's sedated. Not in pain, they believe. I haven't asked if pneumonia is like drowning. They can't say when, but the swathe of the curtains suggests that there won't be a tomorrow for us, suspended on the third floor of the hospital. I open the porthole in the side of the incubator and fold my fingers around a swollen arm: Jennifer's arm.

I let go of the doll. At that moment it seemed the most heroic of gestures, the doll instead of my sister, a choice that had to be made in an instant. Let the doll drown, let it not be Emily.

Splash.

The ferryman slowed his pulling, but the momentum of the boat pushed us past my bobbing doll. 'On the way back, sweetheart,' he said to me. 'On the way back, I'll see if I can't just scoop her out.' But everyone could see that she was drifting in the lazy current, downriver, towards the weir.

'What was her name?' Emily asked rubbing her arm where I'd clamped it tight.

I leaned close to her ear and whispered it there.

Dad was waiting on the bank. He looked like he was going to say something, but he stopped as he registered Emily's misery-pinched face. 'What a day,' he said wearily. 'The sooner we get home the better.'

He set off at marching pace. Every so often he stopped and turned around. 'Come on,' he called. 'Hurry up.' He broke into a run as we neared home and saw the ambulance outside the house. My brother had been born while we were out. *James – 7 pounds 3 ounces*, Dad wrote later on a piece of paper that he taped to the front door.

But even the sight of the ambulance couldn't hurry Emily. She dawdled along the road, nursing her upset. And all the way to the front door, her sombre lips mouthed, 'Poor, poor Jennifer.'

Under covers

Carol's bra is spread-eagled in the hedge like a monstrous, albino bat. The wind has blown it off the washing line and tossed it onto the wispy fingertips of the leylandii, where it reclines in a sprawl of wire, hooks and corralling lace. Despite her best efforts, she can't reach it. Her washing basket is full of dry laundry. She has removed the pegs from the line and placed them in their little bag. But she can't go back indoors until she has retrieved the fugitive bra. People might see it.

Earlier on, she hung the little peg bag from the washing line and listened to the pegs crackle as she slid it along. Some people place washing on their lines in an untidy jumble, without even pairing the socks, but Carol hangs things out in an orderly manner, beginning at the far end of the washing line with undergarments and tights. These are followed by blouses, skirts and cardigans, and finally larger items, such as sheets. Sheets are her favourite. They wriggle and flap, squirm and wave until they are marinated in the season. Summer sheets are best. Their dusty warmth reminds Carol of sandy beaches and she brims with nostalgia, recalling the selected highlights of seaside trips with her sons. Sandy sandwiches, sun burn and fear of death by drowning have been consigned to the dustbin of memory.

Carol looks around the garden for something to help her reach and dislodge the bra. The tools are locked in the shed, and she doesn't want to go back into the house while her bra is exposing itself to the neighbours. Her happiness is stacked in slender, ordered discs, like a packet of Rich Tea biscuits. Unexpected events upset her. Every day she does a wash. There is always plenty to fill the machine because almost everything in her house is covered in washable fabric. The toilet roll is masked by a knitted pig, the toilet lid is embraced by a cross-stitched cover and the bottom of the bath is concealed by an antibacterial, machine-washable, anti-slip mat. The carpet in the lounge is hidden by a beige rug, the dining table lurks under a daily rotated cloth and the sofa is veiled by a patchwork throw. Hot-water bottles are wrapped in furry animal cases, hard-boiled eggs wear knitted warmers and even her occasional bottle of wine must get dressed in a seasonal sweater before standing on the table. Plates are buried under lacy doilies and the teapot is insulated by a cosy, while Carol's arms and legs are consistently wrapped in cardigans and flesh-coloured tights. Today's wash is white, full of underwear and table cloths. It has dried quickly in the wafting breeze, a fact that would usually make her happy.

*

Next door, Sophie and Louisa lie on parallel beds, Swiss-rolled by duvets and yawning like lions. They've slept through breakfast and lunch, and landed somewhere in the middle of the afternoon. Louisa unravels herself and kicks her duvet away. She knuckles her eyes and remembers the whispered conversation that kept them awake so long. Her friendship with Sophie is new and needs the reinforcement of disclosure. Last night they exchanged confidences like gifts, feeding each other small nibbles of truth: 'I used to fancy Matt Jones', and 'I used to suck my thumb'. Louisa hasn't told Sophie about what happened with Matt Jones, yet. She hasn't said anything about following him into the garden at a party, about the way his tongue slugged in and out of her mouth, the way his spit dribbled down her chin. She hasn't talked about not knowing how to breathe or mentioned his busy hands, patting her down in a way that reminded her of the time she'd been body-searched at the airport. Eventually he uncoupled himself with a great slurp. 'What's up with you, then?' he said. 'You frigid or something?'

Louisa kneels up and crawls to the end of the bed where she can lift a small corner of curtain to eye the weather. Outside, April is blustering about, swiping at trees and giving her mum's washing a walloping. 'Come and look at this, Sophie,' she giggles.

Sophie is lost in the swirl of a chasmal yawn. Her hair orbits her head in an orange cloud. She waves a hang-on-a-minute hand at Louisa.

'Come on. Quick! You're going to miss it.'

Sophie gets out of bed and shuffles to the window.

'Look!' Louisa points. 'It's Mrs Evans from next door. Her bra's blown away. It's stuck in the hedge.'

Sophie crouches next to her friend so as not to be seen. The tips of her bright curls tickle Louisa's cheek. They stare at Mrs Evans for a moment, watch her reach up and fall short.

'Look at the size of it! It's enormous,' Sophie giggles.

'She's got massive bazongers, that's why.'

'Bazongers?' Sophie laughs.

'Bazookas, hooters, knockers!' Louisa sniggers. 'Tits, baps, breasts!' She can feel herself beginning to unravel; a coil of Matt Jones-related worry starts to spin out of her chest like cotton from a bobbin. 'Airbags, torpedoes, jugs!' she continues. 'Boobs, melons, speed bumps.'

'Stop it,' Sophie gasps. 'I'm going to wet myself.'

Mrs Evans reaches up again and both girls are mesmerised by the scalloped sway of her upper-arm flesh. Louisa glances at her own, tightly wrapped arms. 'I am *never* going to have arms like that,' she announces confidently.

'I bet it's the first time her underwear's ever been in a hedge,' Sophie says.

And they burst into a fresh whirl of laughter.

*

A long time ago, before bras were allied to absence and excavation, Carol might have been amused by runaway underwear. Back then, she used to read romantic fiction. It was a habit that began when the boys were small and there seemed to be more *ever after* than *happily* about her life. She would pop into the charity shop on London Street and buy the second-hand romances for a few pence each. Then she would lose herself in an exciting world of millionaire business men and exotic holidays. She didn't tell anyone about her romance habit. She was embarrassed of the stories' heaving bosoms and thrusting manhoods. She hid the books in the bottom of her wardrobe and, after a while, in bin bags in the loft. She was more bored than unhappy. There was only so much housework she could do, and as the boys got older, they required less and less mothering. She filled the gaps with romance.

Boris was a good husband. He was kind, straightforward and a hard worker. But he referred to making love as 'how's your father' or 'slap and tickle', and he would say 'wey hey' and 'phworrah' if he happened upon her in her underwear, even after the boys had left home. He commentated on their sexual relations like a football pundit until she told him not to – his Yorkshire accent stopped her from pretending that he was sheik of an imaginary country in the Far East or an Italian Count – and he had to be content instead with a post-match report, sitting up in bed afterwards like Des Lynam, smoothing his moustache and reviewing his selected highlights. Sometimes she enjoyed going to bed with him, but she always felt shy about it afterwards. The next day she would watch him glugging soup at the dinner table and remember his enthusiastic harrumphing, the meaty, schlepping report of his penis, and it all seemed rather ridiculous.

Once he said, 'Kiss me like you've never kissed me before – go on, say it to me.'

'Oh, all right,' she replied. 'Kiss me like you've never kissed me before.' She closed her eyes and waited for his kiss. A tiny part of her imagined the possibility of being swept into his embrace, stretched over his arm and kissed with a passionate but tender fury she had only read about. But he clamped his mouth around her nose and wormed the tip of his tongue into her left nostril. She pushed him hard in the chest and he stepped back, laughing.

'Bet you've never been kissed like that before,' he said.

Occasionally he did something romantic. Once he copied 'Shall I Compare Thee to a Summer's Day?' into a greetings card and wrote, 'That's you that is!!' underneath. A week before she had her left breast removed, he wrote her a letter. She keeps it in the drawer of her bedside cupboard. When she reads it, she can't help but picture Boris; the idiosyncratic underscores sit like moustaches underneath the words he chose to emphasise.

Dear Carol,

On the radio this morning they said that no one writes love letters any more, so I thought I'd have a go. Even with one headlight out, you'll still be <u>smashing</u>. You keep everything so <u>clean</u>. Your Yorkshire puddings are the <u>best</u> I've ever tasted. When I come home and you've been baking, the house is warm, you are in the kitchen and your face is a bit <u>pink</u> – it makes me want to kiss you.

Love,

Boris.

After the surgery she stopped reading romantic fiction. And she stopped taking her bra off in front of Boris. The usual 'how's your father' forays occurred, but she always kept herself covered. Perhaps it was around that time that she started covering up other things too; it helped to keep her crocheting, knitting, sewing hands busy. She got used to the scar and the rucked-up pucker of her freshly-soldered skin. It was the other breast that bothered her, dangling jollily, as if it didn't know yet; it left her feeling unbalanced, it was about as much use as a solitary shoe and, although she tried not to, she wondered if there were lethal secrets concealed in its ducts and lobules.

Boris retired a year after her operation. Not long after, he booked a surprise, off-peak break in Cornwall. On the last evening they went out to dinner. Carol wore a pretty, halter-neck dress with a mohair cardigan to ward off the chill of autumn. Afterwards, they drove to the coastal path at Gunwalloe. It was a dark night. The moon was covered by a constellation of cloud, but the walk was an easy one, down narrow lanes, tunnelled by tall hedges.

'Look, love.' Boris cleared his throat. 'I've been thinking . . . I'm not very good at this sort of thing. So I thought I'd borrow someone else's words. *Let me not to the marriage of true minds,*' he began.

As he delivered the poem, Carol tight-roped between laughter and a spiky emotion that poked her throat. Once she got over the urge to laugh, she recognised that his recitation was the most romantic thing she'd ever heard. She felt as if she was in a scene from one of the novels she used to read, even though they never featured plump, middle-aged, single-breasted women. When he finished, she didn't say anything. They stood together in the darkness, listening to the sea break in the distance, and then he kissed her. As she kissed him back, he slid the cardigan down her arms. She was a little surprised when he slipped a finger into the side of her dress, and under the edge of her bra. She stood very still as he explored the knotty verge of scar tissue.

'There you are,' he said. '*Love is not love which alters when it alteration finds.*'

Standing in the garden, Carol wishes Boris could see her bra, stranded in the hedge. It would make him laugh.

She cases the area once more, in search of a solution and notices the washing-line prop.

The girls watch Mrs Evans fishing for her bra.

'She'll never do it,' Sophie says. 'Is there someone who can help? Does she live by herself?'

'Her husband's dead.' Louisa shrugs. 'He died ages ago. It was like, seven years ago or something, at least.'

'Was he fat, too?' Sophie asks. She tucks a spray of marigold curls behind each ear in order to better observe the old woman's struggle.

'Not really. But he had a big, fat moustache. Like a hairy caterpillar.'

'Gross. Imagine being kissed by someone with a moustache.'

Louisa thinks about being kissed by Matt Jones; the thought is definitely grosser than Mr Evans's furry moustache.

'I can't imagine her kissing anyone, can you?' says Sophie.

Louisa considers Mrs Evans for a moment. 'Not really.'

'Maybe she had a sexless marriage.' Sophie laughs. 'Perhaps she's never done it.'

'She must have. She's got two sons. They come and visit her sometimes.'

'Ew. Can you imagine?' Sophie uncrouches and strikes a pose in front of the window. 'Oh, Mr Evans, don't rumple my apron! I'm trying to wash the table cloths! Stop it, you'll ladder my pop socks!'

'Get down! She'll see you,' Louisa hisses.

'No, Mr Evans, you may not remove my slippers. I'm frigid—'

'Don't be tight.'

'Oh, come on. Look at her! Mr Evans, you're creasing my pleats!'

Louisa is suddenly unsure about Sophie. 'I bet she wasn't frigid when she was younger. People just say stuff like that for the sake of it.'

'Get you! Sticking up for that—'

'Stop it.' Louisa's words unfasten their tentative friendship, leaving it in two pieces like a split end.

Sophie moves away from the window. 'I'm going to the loo,' she huffs.

But Louisa stays on the end of the bed, peeping out through the gap in the curtains. She watches Mrs Evans retrieve the bra and quickly bury it in the waiting washing basket. Then she crawls back into bed and snuggles into a spool of duvet. She closes her eyes and imagines kissing a boy warmly, expertly. The imaginary boy brushes her jaw gently with the tips of his fingers, just like sexy men do in films. And Louisa smiles as she hides under the covers.

Love: terms and conditions

The photograph in my parents' hall is a lie, a counterfeit memory they forged when I was small. Despite their efforts, I can see the truth of my childhood in its pixels. Every time we visit, I am compelled to examine it. Last time we visited, it was Boxing Day. As we waited on the doorstep, I cautioned the children to be on their best behaviour. I reminded them of the rules, explained the consequences of contraventions, and justified the effort required to achieve acceptance.

'Be polite. Eat all of your dinner, and don't ask too many questions.'

'Yes, Mum,' they chorused.

My mother opened the door. 'My favourite grandchildren!' she exclaimed, presenting her cheek to them.

'We're your only grandchildren, silly,' Martha giggled.

'I really don't like kisses, Nanna,' Adam said, as he always does.

'It's true,' I vouched, hoping that she would let him off. 'He won't kiss me, either.'

'No Christmas presents if you don't kiss me,' my mother said.

'Okay then, Nanna.' Adam shrugged and smiled at her. 'Mum and Dad got me an iPod and that's all I really wanted. Merry Christmas.' He squeezed past her sentinelling form, into the house.

'Do I *have* to kiss you?' Jonathan asked.

'Yes,' my mother said.

'One, two, three . . .' He gave her a lightning-quick peck. 'You're like the gatekeeper in a fairy tale, Nanna,' said Martha. 'People have to pay you to get in, with kisses. You should say, "You cannot pass unless you kiss the ugly, wicked witch." And then your kisses could turn everyone into stone and—'

My mother stood to one side and Martha raced down the corridor without offering payment. In an attempt to make up for the children, Chris bestowed a generous, smacking kiss as he stepped inside.

'If they saw you more often . . .' I apologised, as I proffered my lips.

'It's such a long way to drive,' my mother said as she closed the front door, consigning the distances she and my father drive during their transatlantic holidays to an entirely separate category of travel.

I followed her down the hall until I reached the photograph. I stopped to look at myself, aged five, standing in the back garden on a wintry day. I'd pestered and pestered to be allowed outside to play in the fine scatter of snow and eventually my mother gave in. She packed me into my red snowsuit, fastening the zip so high that it caught my throat. Then she escorted me outside and positioned me on the patio. My eyes were awash with unshed tears as my father called, 'Say cheese.' Afterwards, when I wanted to play, they said it was too cold and made me come straight back indoors. They have forgotten this. It is something, along with a horror of compulsory kisses and the nettley prickle of elderly relatives' tissue-paper cheeks, that has been unremembered. They refer to the photograph as 'that lovely picture of you having fun in the snow'.

As I looked at my five-year-old self, forced into a scarecrow stance by my marshmallowing outfit, I wished, not for the first time, that I could stretch an arm into the picture, unzip the snowsuit, kiss the nipped throat better, and say, 'Off you go, sweetheart. Go and have a big, messy roll in the snow.'

Martha interrupted my thoughts. 'What are you doing?' she asked as she trundled down the corridor.

'Just looking at this old picture of me.'

'What were you like when you were a little girl, Mummy?'

I thought about it for a moment. 'I was good.'

She reached her arms around the top of my leg and hugged me, hard. 'You are the beautifullest lady in the planet and the land,' she consoled. 'And Nanna says to tell you that the lunch is getting ruined.'

There were five different vegetables at lunch.

'I don't like green beans, thank you, Nanna,' Jonathan said.

'They're good for you,' my mother responded.

'I know, but they squeak in my mouth and they make me shiver.' His eyebrows rummaged for a suitable expression while he laughed nervously, 'He-he.'

'You'll get what you're given, sonny-Jim,' she said as she ladled green beans onto his plate. 'There aren't any fussy eaters in this house.'

'We're not fussy, Nanna,' Martha piped up. 'We eat spaghetti Bolognese, carbonara, fricassee, macaroni cheese and chicken fajitas. Do you like all of—'

'Eat your lunch,' my father interrupted her.

Jonathan desperately tried to make eye contact with me, seeking permission to leave his beans. I pretended that I hadn't noticed, but Chris leaned across the table. 'Don't worry about the beans, Jonno,' he said. 'I hated them when I was younger, too. Love them now though, yum.' He speared a mound of Jonathan's beans with his fork and held them up in a toast to my mother.

Outside, tiny grains of snow began to speckle the patio. I stared out of the dining-room window as they scattered like crumbs, and my father began to talk to Adam about university.

'Oh, that's years away,' Chris interjected.

'I don't want to go to university,' Adam said.

'Your mum went to university. Grandad will be very disappointed in you if you don't go,' my father wheedled.

'You *are* Grandad,' Martha pointed out. 'Do you mean that *you* will be disappointed, Grandad?'

'Yes, of course that's what Grandad means,' my father huffed.

'Well, I don't want to go, anyway,' Adam said. 'And Mum says I don't have to. I'm probably going to be a referee. I'd like to be a professional footballer, but it's not likely cos I haven't been signed yet. Look! It's starting to snow.'

'Can we go outside, after lunch?' Jonathan asked.

'Yes! And build a snowman.' Martha smacked her hands together.

'There's not enough snow for that.' Chris laughed.

'It's freezing out there. You'll catch your death,' my mother said as she scowled a full-stop frown at Martha.

'We'll wrap up warm,' Jonathan assured her. 'Don't worry about us, Nanna. We're tough!'

'You'll make a terrible mess.' My mother shook her head irrevocably.

'We'll be very careful,' Adam promised.

'I said, no.'

'No you didn't, Nanna. She didn't say no, did she, Grandad?'

'Yes she did,' my father insisted. 'Don't argue with your Nanna, Martha.'

There was Christmas pudding with cream for afters, but the children wouldn't try it. The boys refused politely and thanked my mother for making it. 'I think raisins look like spiders, Nanna,' Martha explained. 'Little, dead spider's bodies with the legs pulled—'

'Don't be silly!' my mother said. 'This is *Nanna's* Christmas pudding. Who's going to give it a try? One of my favourite grandsons? My favourite granddaughter? No? You're not at all like your mummy, she always ate everything. Whoever tries it can have a big kiss.'

The children had ice cream and sprinkles, and they remembered to ask if they could leave the table when they finished.

'Wait,' my mother said, pointing at Martha's bowl. 'You haven't eaten all your sprinkles.' She picked the bowl up and scraped the stray sprinkles and a residue of melted ice cream onto a spoon. 'Open wide,' she instructed Martha, whose surprised mouth automatically gaped. 'Good,' she said. 'There are starving children in Africa.'

I spun around in my chair to give Adam a look, but I wasn't quick enough. 'Name two,' he said.

'What?' my mother asked.

'Did you mean "pardon", Nanna?' Martha wondered.

'Name two of the starving children,' said Adam. 'Mum says it for a joke sometimes. That thing about starving children is silly. Over-eating isn't going to help children in Africa. We all say, "Send the food to Africa, then," and things like that. For a joke.'

After lunch the children opened packets of socks and underpants, and finally a large bar of chocolate each.

'Thank you for the socks,' Martha said. 'I've got *hundreds* now.'

Jonathan opened his bar of chocolate and took a large bite out of it.

'You're not going to eat it all in one go?' My father asked, mesmerised by Jonathan's munching chops.

In the car on the way home I thanked the children for being good.

'You're welcome,' they answered: cheeky, greedy and precocious respectively, according to my parents' whispered exchange as we said our goodbyes.

'We're always good,' Martha said, and I heard the boys murmuring agreement as I fiddled with the radio.

'I ate everything except for the green beans.'

'And I told Grandad all about the referee course.'

Chris chuckled quietly as the children listed their virtues. They have grown up in a family where love doesn't track a base rate of obedience. There are no Terms and Conditions to our affection, which has left them utterly unprepared for the measured, auditing love of their grandparents. 'They've got no idea, have they?' Chris whispered, laughing softly. It's all right for him, his parents are dead.

Later that night, when the children were finally asleep, it snowed fat, butterfly flakes. They flittered into our garden like a plague of – cabbage whites. I'd never seen snow like it.

'Let's go outside and build a snowman,' I said to Chris.

'Been there, done that.'

'Come on, I've always wanted to.'

He smiled at me and carried on watching television.

I built the snowman in the front garden. Snow tumbled over me, settling on my head and shoulders. The air was thick with it, muffling everything into silence. Neighbours saw me as they drew their curtains before going to bed. They stared. I waved, bashfully at first, and then with an enthusiasm born of freezing wet extremities and shivery sniggers. It was snowing so heavily that tracks left by my enormous snowball were packed with fresh snow every time I returned to the start of my circuit. When the ball was as high as my waist I couldn't push it any more. I left it next to the garden wall and began again. The snow lifted in a cotton-wool carpet, Swiss-rolling like turf. I picked up the second, smaller ball and placed it on top of the first. Then I whirled a third snowball to add to the others. The snowman was as tall as me. I knelt down and pushed the surrounding snow into the hollows of his body until he rose up out of the ground, as if he had legs. He didn't balance, he stood. I dressed him in a red, sequinned cowboy hat from the pound shop – Martha's Christmas present to me – and a green woolly scarf. I gave him a carrot nose, black grape eyes and I wedged a banana skin into a smiling mouth with the help of cocktail sticks. My first snowman.

The snow was still falling, planting icy kisses on my nose and cheeks when I lay down next to the hedge on a drift knoll and made a snow angel. Chris knocked on the window and made shivering gestures. I waved. I hadn't realised that I had always wanted to lie in the snow, that a small part of me had been patiently waiting to be filled with cold, damp happiness.

I stumbled into the house, cold-clumsy and giggling. 'Let's wake the children up,' I said as Chris tutted at the trail of snow that stalked me. 'It'll make up for earlier, and this is the *real* stuff. Imagine being woken up in the middle of the night and your mum telling you that you can go out and roll in the snow.'

'I don't think . . . there's no need . . .' his words faded as I raced up the stairs, snowing on him as he quietly followed.

I burst into each of their rooms. 'Wake up! Who wants to come outside and play in the snow? You've never seen snow like it! It may never snow like this again!'

'Oh go away, Mummy,' Martha groaned.

Adam and Jonathan dragged themselves out of bed, deigning to look out of the window.

'Look what I made. He looks just like *The Snowman*.'

'No he doesn't,' said Adam.

'Why don't you come outside for a bit while it's still snowing?'

'You'll let us go out in the morning, won't you?' Jonathan yawned.

'Yes, but don't you want to come right now? Look at the snowman. Do you think he might come to life?'

The snowman stood in the front garden expectantly, smiling his banana-skin grin at us, a lone figure in the unfamiliar, white landscape. The boys stared at me for a moment, rolled their eyes at each other and stumbled back to bed.

I went downstairs and switched the lounge light off. I opened the curtains and looked at my snowman. He was a model of contentment; amenable and compliant, entirely comprehensible, his perpetual happiness secured by a pair of well-positioned cocktail sticks. My parents would have loved him.

In the morning, I watched through the lounge window as the children undid my snowman. At first it was a matter of improvement and rearrangement, but it quickly turned into something else; he was dismembered, razed, annihilated. And then they began again. The three heaps of his carcass were remodelled, enhanced and cast into fresh creations.

'Didn't you like my snowman?' I asked as they tumbled back into the house, frozen pink and snow-sparkled.

'It was okay,' Adam admitted. 'But it was a bit boring. My alien's better.'

'So is my snow bear,' said Jonathan.

'Yours was nice, Mummy. But I wanted to make my own.' Martha flopped onto the sofa next to me and wrinkled her face into tight pleats of pretend sleep. 'I'm Sleeping Beauty.' She spoke out of the side of her mouth so as not to spoil the appearance of sleep. 'Sleeping Beauty falls in love with a handsome person. And she's a mermaid. She has three days to make him kiss her. She doesn't even tell her dad about it. Do you like my snow dog? Is he your favourite? Yesterday Grandma said I was her favourite granddaughter. Do you love me the most? Am I your favourite?'

'Your snow dog is lovely.' I said. 'And I love you all the same.'

Adam laughed. 'Ha! We all know who your favourite is,' he said.

'I don't have favourites, Adam.'

Martha started to snore, softly at first, then with intensifying piggyness. Jonathan watched Adam, waiting for him to reveal the name of the favourite child, hoping it was him, suspecting that it wasn't. His eyes darted between Adam and me. I felt like a contestant on a talent show with the camera trained on my face, preparing to examine the truth of my reaction.

Adam cleared his throat before announcing, 'Obviously, it's me!'

Martha gave an extra-loud snort. Jonathan wore his

hurt around his eyes, like glasses. He blinked furiously and shivered his eyebrows.

'That is not true,' I said.

Martha paused her piggy snores and opened her eyes. 'Go on, Mummy. Measure who is your favourite. It's me, isn't it?'

'No.'

Jonathan looked hopeful again. He smiled at me, then looked down, bracing himself behind the wall of his forehead.

'None of you is my favourite. I love you all exactly the same.'

Jonathan shrugged, as if to say he knew it wasn't him, anyway. Martha gave a strident snort and reclosed her eyes. But Adam heckled me with a loop of, 'Liar, liar, pants on fire,' and he was right. I was lying. I don't love them all the same.

The truth is that I love Adam the most. Adult teeth haphazard his gums like tombstones. He is barely put together: jumbly, slouching, still soft-skinned, trying on opinions, wearing ideas then discarding them like socks. He makes up quizzes.

'How many goals did Wayne Rooney score last season?' he asked once.

'I don't know,' I said. 'Do *you* know?'

'No,' he answered. 'But it was probably about fifty.'

He makes up jokes: Who is the grumpiest player in the

premiership? Peter Grouch. Who is the rudest player in Man United? Wayne Mooney. Who is the cleanest Arsenal player? Van Persil.

His disclosures curl like his free kicks, quickly and before anyone can protect themselves: 'Yes I have got homework. Just a diagram. I've got to label it. It's a big vagina.' 'I don't know why you're being so nice to Jonathan because he's got a sore willy; I've got a hair on my balls.' 'Dad hit his thumb with the hammer. He says he said *Slug in a ditch*, but it sounded more like *Son of a bitch* to me.'

At bedtime he chats to me. These chats are a diversion, a detour from sleep that I allow him to follow in order to experience his search for subjects, his quest for conversation. He nods sagely, pretends an interest in everything I say; even boredom is better than bed. He asks me questions about my childhood and although I discern a lack of interest in the side-to-side of his eyes, in the deliberate creases scaffolded by his eyebrows, I answer. I want him to be interested.

Martha opened one eye, but when she caught me looking at her, she closed it again quickly.

'Are you *sure* that you love us all exactly the same?' Jonathan asked.

And I realised. The truth is that I love him the most. His ears fan like trophy handles, cupping the prize of his face. His lips are gentle. They press regular kisses on my cheeks and forehead and they shuffle about silently as he reads to himself. He makes up sums and marks the correct answers with little tick-flicks of happiness. A nervous laugh attends him like the buzz of a diligent insect. 'I think I'm actually your favourite, Mum, he-he,' he finally managed.

I smiled at him and he came to sit on my knee. The bones of his backside knuckled my thighs, he smelt of skin and fabric softener. 'The favourite child is sitting on Mum's knee, he-he.'

Martha briefly opened both eyes and blew a wet raspberry at him.

He is all arms and legs, stretchy, yet inflexible, no longer able to fold himself small. Of the three of them, he is the most eager to please, the most anxious to be approved of and yet the grumpiest and the most likely to be cruel. 'Yes, your bum does look big in that,' he occasionally says by way of morning greeting. 'Your cooking is *disgusting*,' he accuses me several times a week. 'Of course I *know* it's not a restaurant – the food's too yucky.'

I leaned forward and rested my head on the bony shelf of his shoulder. He squirmed a little, giggled as my chin tickled him, and then jumped off my lap. Martha opened her eyes to see what was going on. She stopped pretending to be asleep, and lifted alternate legs into the air, pedalling an invisible bicycle.

'I like to ride my bicycle,' she sang.

It is also true that I love her the most. When she parts the curtain of her hair, her chin peeps out like the point of a star. There is a dimple as deep as a pencil poke in her right cheek and when she grins it burrows further, arcing like an extra smile. Her hands are still baby-padded and blunt, they pat and stroke with impunity. She is stubborn and unyielding. Once she blew up a crocodile rubber ring. She huffed around the house encircled by green plastic, chastising the grinning creature with her forceful hands. She refused to remove it at meal times, and at bed time I found her lying awkwardly in bed still wearing it. 'I am an explorer,' she said. 'I've finished explorer school and I *must* wear this to my congradulation. No, congradulation *is* what I meant, Mummy.' There are emotions which are still too big for her. There are times when she must clench her teeth and scrunch her face to help the words on their way out: 'Why has Daddy *peeled* off his beard?' 'I don't like these shoes any more. No, they're not too small; they're too *fat*.'

She stopped pedalling her invisible bicycle and began to kick her legs against the sofa. It was probably the rhythmic pounding of her feet that caused Adam to leap up and shout, 'Pile on Mum!' I made a half-hearted attempt to escape and then allowed them to drag me onto the carpet. From my position on the floor I could see the chocked clouds were beginning to sieve a light scatter of snow on the garden.

'This'll teach you to say I'm not your favourite,' shouted Adam.

'You're not the favourite, Adam. It's me, he-he,' Jonathan dared.

Martha oinked at the pair of them.

'Look! It's snowing,' I said. 'Shall we go outside? We could build another—'

'Stop changing the subject,' Adam interrupted. 'Who do you love the most?'

Martha printed her palms over my eyes and pushed hard into the sockets. Jonathan sat on my stomach. 'Surrender,' he shouted.

Adam held one of my legs and removed my sock as he prepared to tickle the truth out of me.

'I love you all,' I shouted above their laughter. 'You're all my favourite. It's true!'

I remembered my five-year-old self, immobilised by the stiff puff of a snowsuit, constrained and compliant, the good girl who buttressed her parents' truth. The children's hollers and whoops dispersed the image. Their weight was mashing, crushing. I wrapped my arms around as many bits of leg, shoulder and foot as I could reach, and I squeezed them tight: my three favourites. I love them because they are not like me. And that's my truth.

The ice baby

It was Winter Solstice in the North Country, and a day as dark as the inside of an eyelid had imperceptibly stretched into night. Jens was supposed to be in the hall with the rest of the villagers, watching the Mayor light the Yule Log, but he'd slipped away. Liv wouldn't notice, he decided. She was cradling their newest nephew, smiling carefully, determined to make a performance of happiness to any who might pity the mother and child tableau in which she was caught.

Jens's reindeer-skin boots crunched along the powdery crust of fresh snow, which glowed yellow in the warm light of his clockwork torch. Tree skeletons crowded either side of the path until he reached the fjord, where a world of slate-darkness and sparkle opened out in front of him. He switched off the torch to enjoy the black of sky and shadow. He looked at the outline of the snow-wrapped mountains piling in the distance and the smudge-light of the moon, reflected in the frozen fjord. He sat down on a hump of snow-covered rock. He could breathe properly here. The air sliced in and out of him, cauterising his thoughts, making things clearer, cleaner and less complicated. In the spring when the fjord melted, he and Liv would leave the island and travel to town. They would visit the hospital there. At the hospital pieces of both of them could be mixed up and made into a baby. Lots of people did it. Liv didn't want to, but he would persuade her.

On the way back to the village hall, his torch caught the edge of something slightly off the path and he paused to stroke light over it. He was familiar with feather ice and candle ice, with aufeis sheets and pancake ice. He'd even seen ice discs once as a boy; he'd watched the thin, perfect circles spinning like CDs in the slow-moving river. But he'd never seen anything quite like the piece of ice at the side of the path. Perfectly round, and slightly larger than a football, it was like a giant, glass hailstone. He knelt in the snow and ran his gloved hands over it. He gave it a tentative push. It was heavy, but manageable. He put the clockwork torch in his jacket pocket, lifted the ice ball up to his stomach and walked slowly and carefully along the familiar twists of the path home.

He hefted the ice ball straight to his workshop, where he examined it in the fluorescent-bright light. He unlatched his toolbox and felt the familiar squirming of creativity in his stomach, the twitch of his hands, and the casting of his thoughts. While he'd been carrying the ball he had wondered how it might feel to finally see Liv expanding with their child. To see her moving slowly and carefully through the snow. And that was when he'd decided. As he walked around the sphere of ice resting on his work bench, he pretended to consider other possibilities, but he already knew what was inside it, just as he did when he sculpted wood. And he was right. Every chisel was perfect. When it was time to use the knife, it was as if he was following existing perforations in the ice. It seemed that he was breaking the baby free rather than making her. He sculpted fine lines and decorative cuts across her forehead, knuckles and toes with a V-tool. And then she was finished. The thing he wanted most in the world. She was perfect: diamond bright, and flawless. The most wonderful creation he had ever crafted.

Liv saw the ribbon of light shining under the workshop door when she returned from the Yule celebrations. It was just like Jens to retreat into work rather than face up to the discomfort of another family birth. She was about to knock on the door when she heard a strange sound. It was a cry, but the pitch of it was extraordinary, like the shattering of glass, a tinkling, splintering explosion. She opened the door without knocking. Jens was standing by his work bench holding something wrapped in his coat. The table was shiny-speckled with splinters of ice and trickling puddles.

'What've you got there?' she asked as the jagged crying began again.

'Shh,' Jens whispered. 'Look.' He parted the edges of the coat bundle, and lifted it towards Liv. She stared at the glassy baby as it wriggled and cried.

'What have you done?'

'Made us a baby. Made the thing we want most in the world.' He smiled. 'Isn't she beautiful? Let's call her Asta: it means love.'

Liv took the proffered baby and rocked her gently in the cradle of Jens's coat. 'She's like glass,' she said. 'It's as if she's from an old tale, from the old world of ice, Niflheim.'

'Isn't she lovely?'

Liv felt the cold of Asta's back creeping through the layers of Jens's coat and her own jacket sleeve. 'She's freezing.'

'Don't worry about that.' Jens wafted his hand at her in a return-of-serve, I-don't-care gesture. 'I can't believe I made her. Look at her toes! Aren't they tiny? And look at her ears. All the curly, foldy bits – they're like little flowers.'

The cold was beginning to burn Liv's arm. She handed Asta back. 'What will we do with her, Jens?'

He nodded towards a sheet-covered pile in the corner of the workshop. 'Get the baby stuff out,' he said.

Liv pulled the sheet away from the carefully-arranged baby items they had made over the years: a crib, highchair, playpen, rocking horse, and a box of expertly fashioned toys. All crafted for a child who had no existence.

'The crib, fetch the crib. That's right.' He lifted Asta into the crib. 'There.'

'Shall we carry the crib into the house?' Liv asked.

He looked shocked. 'Don't be silly,' he said. 'She'll get hot in there. Fetch me the sleeping bag and some blankets, and I'll sleep out here with her.'

Jens slept in the workshop with Asta all winter. He was happy. His love for Asta zigzagged through his chest like an icicle. He loved her crystal cries and diamond gaze, her cool smile and frosty fingers. During the daytime he placed her in the playpen on a supermarket freezer bag. He talked and sang to her while he and Liv worked. During breaks they wore thick gloves and ski jackets so that they could pick her up. Sometimes Liv looked sad. But Jens was certain she would get used to being a mother. Some women took a while to adjust to the idea, he'd read up on it. Once, Liv kissed Asta without thinking, and Jens had to help peel her mouth from Asta's glassy forehead. Liv cried, which surprised him as it hadn't hurt much.

As the weeks passed Jens's happiness was niggled by the approach of spring. He worried that in its uncovering of the winter, spring may also undo Asta. He remembered Liv's comment about Niflheim and found a volume of Norse mythology in an old box of books. He read about Muspelheim and Niflheim, worlds of fire and ice that combined to create life. As he and Liv laboured in the workshop, fulfilling furniture commissions, he wondered

141

about installing air conditioning. He thought about the internal electrical generator in his clockwork torch and considered whether such a mechanism might fit in Asta's chest cavity, allowing her to keep cool during the summer.

'You can't do that,' Liv said, when he mentioned it to her.

'Why not?'

'We're not living in some fairy tale world. A clockwork baby! You're like the Emperor in "The Nightingale". Asta is not a *real* baby, Jens.'

'What if I order a chest freezer from the internet?' he said. 'If we could just keep her frozen for the summer—'

'King Midas,' Liv interrupted. 'With his golden statue of a daughter. That's what it would be like.'

'Not at all,' he replied. 'We'd wake her up each winter.'

'Sleeping Beauty,' Liv hit back. 'It wouldn't be fair, Jens.'

Spring came early to the North Country that year. By mid-April it was above freezing and Asta began to melt. Jens was unprepared. He retrieved ice packs from the cool box, froze them and placed them in the playpen. He brought the electric fan down from the loft and fixed its bracing blow, but Asta lay limply in the workshop as the temperature increased. If this was one of Liv's fairy tales, he thought, something would happen. He didn't know what, but it would be *something*. He thought the thoughts that parents of dying children think, he made the impracticable bargains that parents make, yet all the while Asta continued to melt in the warmth. And as she melted it seemed to Jens that her glassy face was streaked with tears.

'Look.' He held Asta up so that Liv could see.

'It's spring,' she said. 'What did you think would happen?'

'Don't you care at all?'

Liv studied him carefully. 'Yes, of course I do. I care that you're upset. But she isn't a *real* baby.'

'She is to me.' He shooed Liv out of the workshop. Asta was dying, dissolving in his arms. He felt a break at the edges of his heart. He struggled for breath as the fracture fissured, splitting through him like a fault line. He knew he would never feel joy again. It would catch on the cracks and go against the grain of him. Despair raged through his capillaries, tears scorched his cheeks, anger blistered across his forehead and temples. He was boiling hot with sorrow. As hot as Muspelheim, he thought.

Liv dashed out to the workshop when she heard the cries. She found Jens, sprawled in front of the door with a pink, wailing baby tucked under his wilting arm. His lips were blue, his eyes glassy.

'What's happened? Whose is this baby? What's wrong? Get up!'

Jens smiled at her and his watery eyes directed her attention to the baby.

'What? What do you want?' Liv put a hand to his head. He was cold and clammy. 'Are you breathing? Can you hear me?' She ran her hands down his arms and across his chest. He was freezing wet.

'I gave her my heart,' he whispered. 'Hot and cold. I made a life . . .'

Liv made a furious noise that was somewhere between a disbelieving laugh and a wail. The baby stopped crying and looked at her curiously. 'Asta?' Liv lifted the baby out of Jens's arm; she was soft, and warm.

At first Liv felt nothing. She pretended that Jens was in the workshop fulfilling a particularly demanding commission. As spring warmed to summer, she fumed. She seethed as she harvested wild cloudberries, Asta's warm bulk dangling from the baby-carrier. She set herself pointless challenges: if I collect enough cloudberries to make jam, he will come back. If I can keep going until the first snow, everything will be all right again. By the time the snow began to fall in early October, she was indifferent. She held Asta up to the workshop window to watch the floating flakes. Asta was entranced, but Liv stared beyond the snow flurry into the past where Jens survived in memories.

Despite Liv's preoccupation, Asta loved her mother with a whole-hearted, unqualified affection.

'What a loving little girl,' people said.

'She has her father's heart,' Liv replied.

As the winter thickened, love for Asta bound the splinters of Liv's grief. She loved Asta's hearty cries and warm gaze, her merry smiles and exploring fingers. She held her on the rocking horse and listened to the sway of her laughter. She sat her in the highchair and fed her toast fingers, spread with sweet, cloudberry jam. She wrapped her in snug layers and carried her down to the fjord, where Asta liked to sit and watch the ice-hard, winter-sparkle of the water.

It was on the way back from the fjord with Asta one day that Liv had the idea. Now that her grief was tight and hard enough to see past and swallow around, there was space for her imagination to operate. When she got home, she went on the internet and ordered the largest chest freezer she could find. She also ordered enough insulating, aluminised bubble wrap to fashion into several pairs of trousers and shirts.

And so, on Winter Solstice, when a day as dark as the inside of an eyelid had imperceptibly stretched into night, Liv left Asta in the village hall with her extended family and crunched through the deep snow along the path to the fjord. Lighting the way with Jens's clockwork torch, she searched for a ball of ice.

Bodies

Aunt Esther lived in America. She found God there. When I was small I thought that was where He lived. Unfortunately, it seemed that Aunt Esther had found the wrong God. I imagined her thumbing through the Yellow Pages, trying various numbers, selecting an incorrect one by mistake. Dad appeared to think that she had done it on purpose. He thought the same about the pregnancy which led to the tragedy of her life. Already a mother of five, she found herself expecting again in her forties. The baby's name was Michael. He died when he was four. 'And that's what you get,' Dad said sagely when relating the story.

People got all kinds of things for not living the way Dad thought they should: illness, divorce, badly-behaved children, every kind of personal calamity you could imagine. 'The world is full of tragedy,' he said, shaking his head sadly, as if the world was nothing to do with us.

The fact that people everywhere were beset by tragedy gave my mother a great deal of purpose. Tragedy spurred her into frenzies of housework and bursts of hymns: *This is the day that the Lord has made, let us rejoice and be glad in it!* Gratitude was her shield. She hid under a tortoise shell of appreciation, hoping to divert God's attention and consequently suspend the long-imagined, anxiously-anticipated tragedies of her own life. 'We're so lucky,' she would say after something particularly dreadful had happened to someone else's family. 'We're so blessed.'

'It helps when you're living right,' Dad used to reply, which made me feel pleased for us and a little worried for everyone else.

Tragedy meant piles of cut flowers wrapped in soggy newspaper on the kitchen table awaiting Mum's arranging fingers. Tragedy reeked of yeast and furniture polish. It meant trays of raspberry buns and spice loaves wrapped in cling film, accompanied by sympathetic notelets addressed in Mum's hesitant, spidery hand.

Aunt Esther had beautiful cursive writing. When Dad first started to say that she had gone loopy, I thought he was talking about her coiling letters. She sent sporadic postcards as if she was on an extended holiday. She had been sending them since long before I was born. Mum kept them in a shoe box under the bed. There was one of the Grand Canyon with the word *Amazing!!* written on the back. Another showed the Hoover Dam and was accompanied by a scrawled *Wowzers!!* Aunt Esther liked to use exclamation marks. They waved from the backs of the postcards like little arms. Single exclamations gave a thumbs-up, like The Fonze. Double exclamations made me picture Aunt Esther with her arms above her head streaming down a rollercoaster track. Dad disproved of exclamation marks. 'The most amazing sentence ever written is: "In the beginning God created the heavens and the earth." And if that doesn't need an exclamation mark, nothing does,' he said.

Every Christmas Aunt Esther wrote a proper letter and enclosed a photograph of her family. These letters and pictures were also kept in the shoe box under the bed. Her first five children were born within seven years of each other and each child's name echoed the initials of her husband Billy-Ray: Bettie-Rose, Benny-Roy, Bailey-Rane, Billy-Reed and Becky-Ruth. Aunt Esther must have moved around a lot because none of these annual photographs seemed to have been taken in the same place. One year the family were pictured wearing padded coats and bobble hats, standing on a cleared path, a foot of snow on either side of them. Another year they were dressed in shorts and T-shirts, smiling into the camera through teeth that gleamed out from brown, freckled faces. In 1970, the year I was born, Aunt Esther sent a photograph that didn't include Billy-Ray. She mentioned that he had gone away in the accompanying letter, but she didn't say where. In the photograph which she sent at Christmas time in 1975, Aunt Esther was holding a new baby. He was wearing a blue coat. There was no accompanying letter. On the back of the photograph she had scribbled *Surprise!!* It was a whole year before we knew his name.

I was probably five when I first found the shoe box. Perhaps I had gone looking for it after the fuss which followed the surprise of that year's Christmas photograph. I couldn't read the letters, but I loved looking at the pictures and postcards. My favourite was one of Aunt Esther and Billy-Ray standing outside a yellow and green hotel in Las Vegas. They were next to a sign which read 'Baccarat Daily'. When I was old enough to read I asked Dad who Baccarat was. He harrumphed, leaving me to conclude that Baccarat was someone else he disapproved of.

Aunt Esther's most memorable letter arrived during the Easter holidays in 1979. It was definitely Easter because Dad had only recently made us sit in the lounge while he gave the glove presentation. He gave the presentation to us every Easter, but that Easter he gave it twice. Once after he caught Timmy and I playing Holy Ghosts with the freshly laundered bed sheets and a second time after the arrival of Aunt Esther's letter.

I didn't like the glove presentation. Dad would hold up one of his hands and wriggle his fingers saying, 'This is your spirit.' Then he would put the glove on and say, 'The spirit has entered the body.' More finger wriggling ensued before his hand fell flat onto the arm of the sofa: death. He would slide his hand out of the glove and say, 'The spirit has left the body.' There was an extra part that year about how the Holy Ghost was a spirit and did not wear a sheet or say *Whoooo*. I hated it all. My body was not a glove. My body was me. I knew exactly where I lived in my body: on a little platform right behind my eyes. I directed everything from there remotely, like a forklift truck driver. I dreaded the day when I would be peeled, drained and separated from myself, hollowed out like the empty glove.

It was Mum who opened Aunt Esther's unexpected Easter letter and she was soon murmuring, 'What a tragedy.'

I wasn't particularly worried by this. I was used to tragedies. Everyone in the neighbourhood came to our house when they had a tragedy. The tragedies ranged from adultery to flat tyres. Dad helped people eagerly, but he was always disappointed when his ministrations didn't lead to conversion. He didn't want to be popular, he was canvassing for God.

'Listen. Oh listen,' said Mum. 'It's Esther's youngest, Michael.' And she read: '*We couldn't find him and then I thought about the river, well it's more of a deep stream really and he liked to play there, but he knew he mustn't by himself.*'

She stopped at this point, mindful of my presence. Little pigs have big ears was one of her favourite sayings. But I know what the letter said next:

And I ran faster than I knew I could and he was in the stream

and I pulled him out and hollered for the kids and blew in his mouth.
He was wet and I was wet and I was yelling and walloping his chest,
but it was too late. God must have needed him more than I did. The
Requiem Mass was beautiful. I enclose a photo. He looks so peaceful.
Pray for us won't you, and write me so I know you've got this letter.
Esther.

There were no exclamation marks. I read the letter
while Mum wasn't looking: she was spraying pine-fresh
polish on the piano and Dad had retired to the lounge
to compose a reply – Aunt Esther had actually included a
return address. As I slid the letter back into the envelope, I
saw the photograph. I didn't know that some people took
photographs of their dead relatives. It seemed like a very
rude thing to do, like taking a picture of someone without
their clothes on. I instinctively knew that the photograph
would meet with Dad's disapproval. It would come into
the category of things that we mustn't do, like drinking
alcohol and having fun on the Sabbath. I'd never seen
Michael so clearly. His face had always been one of several
smallish circles in the Christmas photographs, fuzzed
with distance and eclipsed by his more exotic-sounding,
double-barrelled siblings. He was lying in a white coffin,
wearing a white shirt, surrounded by white flowers. There
was a graven image of the Virgin Mary propped at the
head of the coffin. The white shirt had a frilly collar. In
real life, Michael might have refused to wear it. It was the
sort of shirt that a little boy would only be seen dead in.

One of Michael's eyes was closed, but the other doll-peeped. I couldn't see it properly. Just a floss of white. Enough to suggest that he might be doing it on purpose. The same thing happened to Dad sometimes when he fell asleep on the sofa on Sunday afternoons, I could see a slice of white as he dozed with one eye open. But Michael was dead with one eye open, which seemed absolutely deliberate and incredibly clever. His mouth was sealed shut in a curl that was not quite a smile. His head pressed into the pillow heavily and his chin tilted forwards so that it was almost touching his chest. It looked as if he might sit up in a moment. His hair was auburn and curly. It was dry. I wondered if Aunt Esther had blown it with the hair drier after she pulled him out of the stream. I was so absorbed in the photograph that I jumped when Dad snatched it from me. 'Stop looking at that picture of your cousin's body.'

'It's a picture of Michael,' I said. But as far as my parents were concerned, he was no longer Michael. He was Michael's body. Dad had called it, 'That picture of your cousin's body.' Yet Michael wasn't flat like an empty glove, he wasn't hollow, he was full of Michael. I could tell.

'What happens if Michael wakes up?' I asked at lunch time.

'People don't wake up after they're dead,' Dad said.

'Will you take a picture of me when I die?' Timmy paused between mouthfuls to find out.

'*We* don't take pictures of dead people,' Dad said.

'Of course not, darling.' Mum gave Dad a look. 'And anyway, you won't die until you are a very old man.'

I looked at Mum and Dad. 'Maybe we will take pictures of *them* when they die,' I said to Timmy.

'*We* don't take pictures of dead people,' Dad reiterated.

'What was wrong with him?' Timmy asked.

'He drowned,' said Mum.

'Yeh, but what was *wrong* with him?'

'Nothing was wrong with him until he drowned,' Mum explained.

'What if he gets hungry?' Timmy wondered.

'People don't get hungry after they're dead,' Dad said.

'Is it cold in the ground?'

'No,' Dad said.

'How do you know?' Timmy persisted.

'Because I do,' Dad replied, which of course indicated to Timmy and me that he knew no such thing.

The Holy Ghosts game was not nearly as fun as our new game, Dead Bodies. Because Timmy was a boy and only slightly older than Michael, he got to be the body. Our back garden was stuffed with flowers in preparation for inevitable tragedies; Mum picked and distributed them when necessary. As it was Easter, Timmy and I had to make do with daffodils, a few tulips and the crocuses that quivered shyly around the trunks of the fruit trees. Timmy lay on the grass next to the fence with his hands clasped across his chest. He peeped out of half-shuttered eye lids. I collected the floral tributes and arranged them around him. It was hard to pick flowers without scissors or shears and sometimes I ended up with fists full of petals, which I duly sprinkled over him. Neither of us had been to a funeral before, but we'd spent enough of our lives in church to imagine what one might be like. I conducted the service, which by rights ought to have been done by Timmy because he was a boy. But I was older and he was dead.

I began with the opening hymn, 'All Things Bright and Beautiful', and found that I knew four out of the five verses quite well. This was followed by a very long prayer with lots of pleading and gratitude in it. It seemed appropriate to say a few words about the dead and I began to offer my tribute to Timmy. By this time he was starting to fidget.

'Timmy was six. He liked trains. He had lots of them.'

'I had sixteen,' Timmy interrupted. 'But that one with the yellow funnel got lost.'

'Shh.' I signalled to him to lie still. 'Timmy's favourite dinner was chicken and rice and his favourite pudding . . . What's your favourite pudding?' I asked.

'Angel Delight,' he said with a giggle.

'Angel Delight. Timmy was quite good and didn't do very much sinning, so he will probably go to heaven and not be punished, though it's hard to say. Look at Job and

God *liked* him.'

'I'm bored,' said Timmy.

'Shh.'

'I've had enough.' He started to sit up.

'Okay,' I said. 'I'll be dead now.'

We swapped places. I lay on the warm grass and closed my eyes while Timmy picked flowers. I didn't peep. I breathed slowly and tried to imagine what it would be like if the ground opened beneath me. Would the soil be wet or dry? Would it crumble or stick? What would it smell like?

Timmy's flower picking was worse than mine. He sprinkled me with torn petals and segments of twigs which he had broken off the fruit trees. He welcomed the congregation to the funeral with the same upside-down, singsong intonation Dad used at church. He opened the service with 'Alice the Camel's got Five Humps' before changing to 'Jesus Wants Me for a Sunbeam' after I gave a deathly cough. He offered a prayer that we had learned from an older boy at Sunday school but never dared to say in front of Dad. 'Rub-a-dub-dub, thanks-for-the-grub.' I pulled a face, but kept my eyes closed. 'Oh, all right.' He tried again, this time asking for a blessing on the sick, the afflicted and the dead that they would get better soon and be at church next Sunday.

I was anxious to listen to his tribute to me, but he was fed up.

'I'm hungry. I can smell raspberry buns. Mum can't post them to Aunt Esther in America, can she?'

I shook my head.

'Then they're for us, for tea. I'm going to lick the bowl.'

He ran back into the house, leaving me lying on the grass. I lay there for a while, shrinking into the space behind my eyes, trickling out of my limbs until all of me was right there on the platform in the hub of my head. I breathed slowly and quietly. I wondered how Michael would breathe and then I remembered that he couldn't. I heard the garden living around me. I was warm and fuddly. I fell asleep.

When I woke up I was sticky and heavy. It took me several moments to crawl out of sleep and back into my body. I blinked into the brightness. My hands were still clasped across my chest, empty until I found the command to move a finger and send the life prickling back into them. As I pushed myself up I saw the criss-cross pattern of grass stencilled on my elbows, and I saw Dad, bent over, peering through a knot in the fence, further down the garden.

'What are you doing?' I called.

'Nothing,' he said and strolled back into the house.

I got up and brushed myself down. I walked to the spot where Dad had been standing. I had to balance on tiptoe in order to look through the knot and into next door's garden. Mrs Rigby was lying on a rug on the grass.

She was as brown and shiny as a sausage. She was wearing bikini bottoms. Her hands were crossed over her chest just like mine had been. I thought that she might be dead. I didn't realise I was holding my breath until she lifted a hand to scratch her nose and the air galed out of me.

Later on, at tea time, I let Dad know. 'It's all right,' I told him. 'Mrs Rigby is alive.'

'I don't know what you're talking about.'

'She looked like she was dead. But it's okay, I saw her move.'

He dismissed me with a wide hand-sweep and asked Mum to say grace. She prayed for Aunt Esther. She asked God to bless our food, thanked Him for our health, and fervently petitioned Him to continue to keep us from harm, in particular drowning. It was quite easy for God to do this because there wasn't a small river, or even a stream next to our garden. There was only Mrs Rigby, lying parallel to the fence, her juicy legs popping out of her bikini bottoms. But Mum probably wasn't thinking about Mrs Rigby as she tucked into a still-warm raspberry bun, determinedly grateful for what she was about to receive.

I will never disappoint my children

She looks like an evacuee, sitting on a chair outside the school office with her lunchbox clutched to her chest. She smiles when she sees you. But it's the sort of exasperated smile that your parents used to give, a smile that speaks of loving you *anyway* and *despite*.

'Sorry,' you mutter to the teacher whose smile also fails its welcome.

You need the loo. You are tomato-faced, sweaty. When you removed your cardigan earlier during the meeting that made you late, you were appalled by the sight of your milky arms and their thick winter coat of flesh; you immediately re-covered them and kept the cardigan on afterwards, in the greenhousing heat of your car.

You hold her hand as you leave the school together. It is warm, stickied by hot classrooms and wax crayons. She tells you a story about a boy called George who might love her. You buckle her into the car seat and listen to more about George.

'He let me use his best eraser in the shape of an aeroplane, and he didn't tig me at playtime . . .'

She doesn't stop talking as you walk around the car to the driver's side. You have a little time before you need to pick up your sons from high school: twenty minutes to counteract your lateness. When you reach the end of the road, you turn right.

'Where are we going?'

'For an ice cream,' you say.

You drive along the coastal road, past wet ripples of sand that stretch for miles. You can't see the sea, but Blackpool is visible in the distance through the quivering heat-haze.

You went to Blackpool once on holiday with your family. Your dad promised to buy everyone an ice cream, a proper one from a shop. He held the shop door open as you spilled inside, sunburned and sand-speckled. He shepherded you into a huddle and made a show of counting everyone, including himself.

'That'll be eight ice creams, please.' He smiled his wide, pumpkin smile, revealing zigzag gaps of absent molars. 'Can you do a discount?' he asked as he emptied the contents of his wallet into his hand. 'No? An extra small scoop for a reduced price, then?'

You reach the roundabout by the pier and turn off into the car park. The fast-food restaurant is enveloped by scaffolding.

'It's closed,' your daughter says firmly, as if she was expecting to be disappointed.

'No, look. The drive-through is still open.'

You pull into a space next to the fabric warehouse.

'What are you doing?'

'I just need to pop into the shop and go to the loo.'

'But you said I could have an ice cream.'

'You can, but I really need the loo first. Let's go quickly.'

She refuses to undo her seatbelt. She leans sideways, drooping out of her car seat like a little drunk. You reach for the seatbelt and your hand knocks into her.

'Ouch,' she exclaims, clutching her face, her neck, her shoulder. She starts to cry.

'Where does it hurt?' you ask. 'I hardly touched you. I'm sorry.'

'Owwww,' she howls.

'Where does it hurt?'

She won't say. She cries heartily, wringing herself out. You lean back in your chair and stare at the pier needling into the distance, pointing towards the far-flung sea.

When she has finished crying you get out of the car and go into the shop. She follows you grudgingly, huffing and puffing up the stairs, sighing heavily each time you pause to allow her to catch up. While you are in the cubicle she peeps the scuffed tip of her shoe under the door. She scowls at you in the mirror as you wash your hands.

You hurry out of the shop and she darts after, stopping as she notices what you have already observed: a long queue of cars snaking up to the drive-through window. You glance at your watch as she exhales loudly.

'I'm really sorry,' you begin.

'If you hadn't gone in that shop . . .'

'We haven't got time to sit in the queue. We'll be late for your brothers.'

'You were late for me,' she says.

You drive away from the beach, over the hump of the Marine Bridge, toward the high school. You turn the CD player on. It's her favourite track, a carnival song about *Alice in Wonderland*. She extends her right leg and switches the CD player off with the tip of her scuffed shoe. Her eyes slice anger at you and she fixes you with a fierce, dredging stare. Then she turns her head, rests it against the passenger window and watches as the wide plane of the beach and the distant view of Blackpool recede.

In Blackpool, your dad handed you a reduced-price ice cream. The tiny scoop topped the cone like a pea on a drum.

'Say thank you,' he prompted.

You zipped your lips tight shut and watched other families order normal-sized ice creams, strewn with sherbet and pink sauce. Your older brothers scooped the ice cream from their cones in a single gobble-lick.

'You haven't said thank you,' he repeated as he marshalled everyone out onto the pavement. 'Are you going to say thank you?'

You shook your head. He tried to take the ice cream from you. He tried to snatch it for a ransom of gratitude, but he knocked it out of your hand and it landed upside down on the pavement.

'I'm sorry,' he said.

You gazed at him through slit-thin, witnessing eyes. Blackpool Tower loomed like an enormous salt shaker, a tram passed in a gust of warm air and you slotted a picture of the scene into the projector of your memory. When I grow up, I will never disappoint my children like this.

On the way home

Rob Turner has done something amazing. He strides along Bridge Road, carrying his jacket over one arm so that people can see. The pavement flocks with noisy, red-faced children as they stream out of the primary school. Rob pauses to stand aside for buggies. He says, 'No problem,' when he is thanked. He raises his bare arm to distracted women in an after-you gesture, and he smiles over the undulating bobble hats. He notices in the hope of being noticed. His college motto is Treat Others as You Would Like to be Treated Yourself. He watches small hands picking noses and itching at the scratch of bobble hats. He observes mittens on strings, fingerless gloves and ear muffs. Despite the cold, he holds his jacket, exposing his left arm as he shepherds children past. 'Go on, then. Off you go,' he says. 'You look like you're in a hurry. S'okay, you go first'.

He feels benevolent, fatherly. The feeling started when the nurse, who was surely old enough to be his grandmother, called him Mr Turner. 'Lie down here, Mr Turner,' she said.

He hadn't realised he would have to lie down. He felt very serious. So this is what it would be like to be ill, he thought, as he leaned into the thick pillow. He hoped there would be time to go back to college afterwards and show his arm to Kate Wilson. He imagined her leaning over it sympathetically, offering to kiss him better. But it was too late now.

'Press this on tight,' the nurse said afterwards, pushing a piece of gauze into the crack of his arm. 'It'll help to stop any bruising.'

Rob pressed lightly.

The juice and biscuits were a surprise. He had been expecting some thanks, but the insistence of, 'Get something inside you,' and the attentiveness of, 'Sit down for a moment and rest,' gave his enjoyment a gravity to be savoured.

Biscuits. Only plain ones, but he helped himself. He deserved them. There should be biscuits, he thought. In fact, there should be better biscuits, like the ones with cows on, or custard creams. He felt appreciated, considered, part of an altruistic group who had eaten National Health Service biscuits. Other people were also eating the biscuits. They were mostly older. Some were chatting. He wanted to join in, but couldn't decide how to begin.

The flow of children reduces to a trickle. Rob's left arm hangs awkwardly, inside-out, in the hope that someone might comment on the white, sticky plaster. Any one of these children could be saved with his blood. Any one of them might have cause to be grateful to him one day and never know who to thank. He briefly empathises with Peter Parker, with Clark Kent and Bruce Wayne, their heroic deeds unacknowledged in everyday life.

He strides on, past the hairdresser's, the pharmacy, the betting shop and the laundrette. He goes into the corner shop. There are lots of biscuits here. Coconut Rings, Party Rings, Pink Wafers, Jaffa Cakes and Jammie Dodgers. He chooses a packet of Bourbon Creams and presents them to the man behind the till, using his left hand.

'Ninety pence,' says the man, whose nametag reads, 'Girish Patel. Can I help you?'

Rob scratches around the sticky plaster for emphasis. A bruise has leaked past its edges.

'You been in the wars?' Girish asks the young lad buying chocolate biscuits.

'I gave blood.'

'Good for you.'

Girish hands the boy his change and watches him put his jacket on as he struts out of the shop. 'I'm going in the back for a bit,' he tells his daughter, Parv. 'Call me if it gets busy.' He brushes through the dangling coloured ribbons, into the store room, catching his hip on the jut of a crate of washing powder. He hobbles on into the kitchen where Amir is waiting with his school reading book.

'Okay, Grandad,' says Amir. 'Ready?'

Girish sits at the table. 'Go ahead, lovely boy,' he says.

Amir has a beautiful voice: high and clear, a laughing voice, a voice that twinkles. *'The Emperor Caligula made mothers and fathers watch their children being executed,'* he reads.

Not long until the end of this horrible book, Girish thinks as he rubs his aching hip.

'Caligula's chief animal-keeper was beaten with chains, day after day. At last the man's leaking brains began to stink so Caligula had him executed.'

Girish shudders. The poor animal-keeper. What a book. Children used to learn from history, now they laugh at it. Amir's bright voice reads on.

'At one dinner he paraded a slave who had stolen some silver. Executioners chopped off the man's hands and tied them round his neck. They made a sign explaining what he had done to deserve it and took him on a tour of the tables.'

Who would do such a thing? Girish adds the question to his growing collection. He is hoarding questions, stockpiling them. His 'Introduction to the Internet' class on Wednesday evenings at the university has not been the antidote he hoped for. There is a poster in the corridor on the way to the computer suite: 'Teaching Singing to Boys and Teenagers,' it reads. 'The Young Male Voice and the Problem of Masculinity: How High Should Boys

Sing?' How high should boys sing? What a question! Here is another problem, something else to ponder and contemplate.

'Why did the Romans have difficulty burying the traitors Drusus and Nero?'

Why is Amir reading this book? Why do boys' underpants stick out of their trousers? How does the writing go right through the centre of a stick of rock? Why do people buy rude birthday cards? How do teenagers balance on skateboards? Girish remembers one of Parv's old books, *American Short Stories*. He read some of them on a quiet evening. There was a story about a man named Kugelmass who ended up stuck in a book, being chased by a Spanish verb. It didn't seem like such a bad thing, Girish thought. Rather a verb than a question mark. He would rather be doing than wondering. Which is why he hesitated in his internet class when the teacher insisted on something fun. The death clock. And now he can't forget it – Tuesday 24th May 2021.

'You've got three hundred and sixty-one million, two hundred and ninety-six thousand four hundred and thirty-nine seconds left to live,' the teacher had chuckled.

He has less time left now, of course.

'Saint Lawrence laughed about his execution. He was roasted on a grill over a fire. After some time he told his torturer, I think I'm cooked now. Eat a slice of me and let me know if I taste good.'

'Dad, can you just pop back in for a minute?' Parv calls through the store room.

'Lovely reading, Amir. Good boy.' Girish strokes Amir's soft head before returning to the shop.

'Do we have any stamps, Dad?' Parv is rummaging in the wrong drawer.

'Please don't go to any trouble,' says the elderly woman on the other side of the counter.

'This is no trouble at all.' Girish smiles. 'What stamps would you like, my dear?'

'How much are six first-class?' asks the old woman, flushed by the attention.

Here is a question Girish can answer.

The little Indian man with the shiny head is anxious to please in a way that makes Betty feel both deferred to and desperately old. He produces the book of first-class stamps and bestows them like a present, reminding her of the croissant she found in the bread bin at breakfast time this morning. It's one of the delights of getting older, the way one's memory can take something, such as the last croissant, conceal it then reveal it, like an unexpected present.

'Thank you,' she says.

There are several people waiting behind her. Now that the little man has appeared from behind the ribboned curtain, the queue should dissipate and take the pressure off her trembling hands. But he goes back through the coloured strips. He must have something important to do. She fumbles with the zip of her purse. She has to put the stamps where they usually go or there is a danger that she will forget she has bought them. The letter is waiting to be sent. It is waiting on the table in the hall, exactly where she placed it so as not to forget it this afternoon. But it is to be expected. It's what happens to everyone from time to time. Remember when the children were small? The times when the washing machine was opened in lieu of the fridge? When journeys up the stairs lead to stupor on the landing, and a trip back down in an attempt to retrieve the tail of the memory? This is just another of those times.

A voice in the queue behind her calls, 'Do you need some help, love?'

'A time machine might be useful,' she jokes as the zipper finally seals the metal teeth. People in the queue chuckle. They seem surprised that she can laugh. Despite the awkward trembling of her fingers, despite the sagging of her skin as if it is already parting from the bones in anticipation of what's to come, she is able to laugh. She can also swear, break wind, pick her nose and belch. But some time after she reached the dizzy heights of seventy, she began to feel compulsorily endowed with benignity, censored into pretending that she has forgotten any pleasures more vigorous than the dunking of a ginger nut in a sugary cup of tea. Reduced to making gentle, brave statements about soldiering on and actually saying, on occasion, the awful words *it wasn't like this in my day*. It's expected and Betty doesn't like to disappoint.

The letter which she left on the hall table is bursting with heroic exclamation marks. She smiled as she drew them at the ends of her sentences. But each mark splits the text like a raised arm, a warning flag. *I'm getting so forgetful! I'm covered in bruises! I don't even know where they come from! They don't really hurt, but I'm like a map of the London Underground! Green, yellow and blue all over me!* The exclamations are little flicks of courage, intended to convey humour in the face of adversity. A celebration of her ability to laugh at the tricks her flagging body is playing on her.

Please don't worry about visiting your old mum! Christmas really isn't too far away! Though it would be lovely to see the children before then, I do understand that you are incredibly busy!

She heads for the door and the rush of cold air. A school boy with blonde hair and blue eyes stands on one leg at the threshold of the shop. His other leg is hovering, not quite touching the grey tiles of the floor. 'Don't you set one foot inside that shop,' a woman's voice calls from behind the door. The boy continues to dangle his leg over the threshold. He catches Betty watching him. His face splits into an irresistible grin. He winks at her. Of all the people in the shop, he has winked at *her*. Betty smiles and gives him her best wink back.

*

'Did you just wink at that old lady?' Julie Cliff asks her son, Billy, as she catches up with him at the door of the corner shop. 'I keep telling you not to wink at people, it's rude.'

'She didn't mind. I think she liked it.' Billy winks at his mother for good measure. He has been practising his winks on all sorts of people. He has winked at his teacher, at the neighbours, at the school crossing patrol man, and yesterday he winked at the doctor in the accident and emergency department when he was asked if he was sorry for shutting his mum's fingers in the car door. The wink undermined his otherwise convincing yes.

There is a carelessness about Billy that bothers Julie. 'Can I have that when you're dead?' he sometimes asks her, as if her eventual death is something to which he is already reconciled. But who will love him if Julie dies? It's not that she thinks herself irreplaceable, more that he is not an easily likeable child, something a mother surely shouldn't notice.

'Treat, treat, treat! I'm going to say it until you get me one. Treat, treat, treat.' He lingers in the doorway of the shop, balancing on one leg, teasing with the other.

'You're in the way, Billy. Move, please.' Julie holds his elbow with her uninjured hand, attempting to guide him away from the doorway, but he falls dramatically to the pavement.

'You pushed me over,' he says, with a wink. 'I can't believe you'd do that.'

'Enough,' says Julie. 'Enough.' Her right hand is bandaged and several knuckles are criss-crossed with fine butterfly stitches. Her middle and ring fingers are fastened together. No breaks, just cuts and bruises. It happened last night after Billy strode out of school. He dropped his lunch box and bag at her feet, grabbed the car keys from her hand, and ran to the car. She chased him. She caught up just as he jumped into the passenger seat. And she extended her fingers as he slammed the door shut. She watched him though the glass before he realised, as she held her breath, before the pain hit. He was laughing.

'You'll be the best mum in the world, if you just buy me one tiny, weenie thing. Just one ickle-wickle thing. Tooty Fruities?' He edges closer to the door of the shop.

'No.' Julie is not budging.

'I hate you,' he says. 'You're the worst mum ever.'

She used to be consoled by his occasional, opposing declarations. *You're the bestest mummy in the whole world and I love you. You're lovely and I want to give you a big hug. You're the best mum, ev-er.* Then she overheard him talking to the dog one day. *You're the bestest dog in the whole world. Let me give you a big hug. The best dog ev-er.* The kindness of his words was lost in duplicate. They seemed like a rehearsal for someone else, an experiment.

'Never mind,' she says. 'Someone had to have the worst mum in the world and it's just your bad luck that it's you. Let's go home.'

There are reminders of Billy all over the house. Even when he's at school it is as if he's secretly tormenting her from a distance. There are scribbles on the walls. He stuffs empty, nicked crisp packets down the sides of the sofa. Sometimes there are plastic spiders hidden under her pillow or inside the bedcovers. When she tried to use the stapler last week, all the staples were upside down, lying like dead insects with their little legs in the air.

'Oh, all right,' he says, finally moving away from the shop doorway. 'All right, I'm coming.' He slips an arm around her waist and rubs his head into her side. 'Is your hand okay?' he asks.

'Yes,' she replies. 'Thank you for asking. It's just throbbing a bit, but it's not too bad.'

'Good.'

She pulls him in closer and lands a kiss on the top of his head.

'Yuck.' He springs away from her side, rubbing his head with the flat of his hand.

'You've got a nit on your mouth, Mum.'

Julie raises her good hand to her lips.

'Made you look, made you stare. Made you lose your underwear.' He laughs and sprints off down Bridge Road, turning after a few metres to give her a wink.

Julie sighs and looks away. She sees a little girl waiting by the window of the corner shop. A quiet, uncomplaining child. She is probably only five or six.

She's wearing glasses. Her lips are looped by a circle of chapped skin and there's a hole in the knee of her grey school tights. Julie glances at Billy as he dashes down the street, and then smiles at the little girl.

Anna Jones does not smile at the lady with the bandaged hand. She waits quietly by the window of the corner shop while Mummy gets money out of the cash machine. Anna is good in both the broadest and slightest sense of the word as it is applied to little girls. She makes no fuss. She is no trouble. There is a hole in the knee of her tights where she fell over at play time. A sharp piece of gravel has arrowed a jab of violet. There are other bruises. Bruises that are pinky, purply, brown and grey. At play times Anna is uncertain. She has no talent for the role-playing games enjoyed by other girls in her class. The boys' games are more straightforward, their rules clearer, fairer: stuck-in-the-mud, tag, British Bulldog, and football. The boys are rough. Play time means bruises. Bruises are hard, and sharp, and quick. They are easier to bear than silences. Some grown-ups describe her as a tomboy, but it might be more accurate to say that Anna is incapable of pretence.

What will she be? She will be a clown for dogs and perform ginormous tricks with sticks and strings of sausages. She said this at school once, and the other children smiled and nodded. It was a good idea. At least it would be, if she was not afraid of dogs. What she would like most of all is to stay at home with Mummy. Forever. But Mummy doesn't like it when she says that. Anna knows this because Mummy's face goes hard, and she says that there is plenty of time to decide; girls can do as well as boys and must do whatever they want to in life. Doing whatever she wants to does not seem to include staying at home with Mummy, although it might include being a chef, but Anna isn't sure.

Mummy is pushing her numbers into the cash machine. Anna can hear them. They sound like the beginning of 'Bobby Shafto's Gone to Sea'.

Bobby Shafto's gone to sea, silver buckles on his knee . . . Bobby Shafto's buckles remind Anna of her bruise. The hole in her tights is quite small. Small enough to stick one finger in. Anna pushes a finger through the frayed wool to give her knee a rub. Tendrils of grey unravel around it.

Mummy finishes at the cash machine. She holds out her hand and then notices the hole. 'Oh, Anna.' The mild rebuke presses a slump on Anna's shoulders. Mummy is disappointed again. 'Wait one second,' Mummy says, and she disappears into the shop.

Anna can see the shop counter through the window. A little man with a shiny head pushes through the dangling ribbon curtain. A boy with velvety, black hair follows after him. The boy climbs onto a high stool and the man pats the boy's knee before turning to serve Mummy. Anna turns back to face the street. Car lights are beginning to shine. Across the road at the bus stop she can see a big boy taking off his jacket. He's showing his arm to the old lady next to him and she watches as the old lady rests her hand on the crease of it for a moment. Further down Bridge Road, Anna can see the back of the lady who smiled at her earlier. She has caught up with her son and they are jogging together, holding hands. It's as if they are running from the street lights as they begin to ping on.

Mummy comes out of the shop holding a paper-wrapped lollypop. 'Don't worry about the tights, sweetheart. That looks sore. Does it hurt?'

'A bit,' Anna admits.

'I know something that always makes people feel better,' Mummy says. She hands the lollypop to Anna. Then she crouches on the pavement of Bridge Road and places winter-cool lips on the exposed cap of Anna's knee where it pokes through the hole in her tights, round as a biscuit.

And on the knobble at the base of Mummy's neck, in the delicate fuzz of hair, Anna plants a soft, dry kiss of her own.

Acknowledgements

I'd like to thank:

Michael Glenday and Rob Mimpriss at the Open University for helping me to realise that it wasn't too late.

All of the teaching staff on the Creative Writing MA at Edge Hill University, especially Daniele Pantano, Ailsa Cox and Robert Sheppard.

Edge Hill's Narrative Research Group.

Amanda Richardson for unwaveringly honest and thoughtful criticism.

Claire Massey and Andrew Hedgecock, the first editors to accept one of my stories.

Jen and Chris Hamilton-Emery for supporting new and emerging writers.

My parents who filled the house with books, told me stories, and tried not to mind when I read at the table.

'Everything a parent needs to know' was originally published as 'Sinking' in *Black Market Review*. 'Just in case' won the MA category of the Edge Hill Short Story Prize and was published in *Mslexia*. An early version of 'The rescue' was published in *The Ranfurly Review* and 'Wooden Mum' was published in *The Yellow Room*. 'Dancing in the kitchen' was published in *Flash Mob: Flax 026*. 'Scaling never' was published in *Dialogue*. 'The baby aisle' was published in *The Delinquent*. 'My burglar' won the Strictly Writing Award and was published at the *Strictly Writing Blog*. 'The countdown' was published in *Mslexia* and 'Bed rest' was published in *PoemMemoirStory*. 'Under covers' was published at *FemaleFirst.co.uk*. 'The ice baby' was published in *New Fairy Tales* and 'On the way home' was published in *The View From Here*.

CARYS BRAY

A Song for Issy Bradley

Shortlisted for the 2014 COSTA First Novel Award
and the Desmond Elliott Prize 2015

Winner of the Authors' Club Best First Novel Award 2015

Meet the Bradleys.

In lots of ways, they're a normal family:
Zippy is sixteen and in love for the first time; Al is thirteen
and dreams of playing for Liverpool.

And in some ways, they're a bit different:
Seven-year-old Jacob believes in miracles. So does his dad.

But these days their mum doesn't believe in anything, not
even getting out of bed.

How does life go on, now that Issy is gone?

'*I cannot remember a time when a novel has seduced me so completely.*'
THE TIMES

'*Wonderful … heartbreaking, compassionate and funny.*'
INDEPENDENT ON SUNDAY

'*Unique … beautifully written … powerful.*'
DAILY MAIL